REVEIWS

Paise for her novel, Headwaters:

*"Much of Headwaters is a physical and spiritual jour-
ney. This mystery includes both a brutal murder and a
magical painterly ending that reads like poetry. Moraczewski's beautiful words are as artful as her paintings. They both
embody the holiness of the female spirit which streams from
the headwaters of the Ranch."*

--Bill Brown, The Cairns, Poems, New and
Selected

ANNA IN PARIS

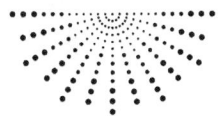

MICHELLE MORACZEWSKI

HOMESTEAD PRODUCTIONS

ANNAINPARIS

FOREWORD

This Book is dedicated to our grandmothers. It's our grandmothers we run to when we escape the tough-love boundaries of our homes. I only began to write this story, as I myself am a grandmother. I write about the wonderful wisdom of youth. Yes, this novella is part memoire, mostly memoire, but the unbelievably simple acceptance of the miracles that surround these two young teens in their travels seems too magical to be true. The wisdom of youth shines here in the uncluttered purity of thought and clear acceptance of life's unfolding as the sisters' step with faith on their journey. The complexity of adulthood and responsibility, clouds our minds from the simple and the miraculous.

It is also a part of travel to bring all of oneself fully into the conversation when sharing stories and ourselves with those who cross our paths. Being fully present, listening and sharing-learning-giving-laughing--as we move through the world. Although those whom we meet we may never see again.

ILLUSTRATIONS

1
ARRIVAL

*R*ose slitted her eyes open to the dim fog of morning.

In a room she didn't recognize, confused about where she was, she shut them and fell into a dark, dreamless sleep. She awoke, eyes wide open, surrounded by a throbbing silence and knew. She was back in Paris.

She jumped up and took in her surroundings. Books stacked tightly in shelves flanked the slender French window. White gauze curtains puffed in the slow breeze through the slightly ajar window that wafted the smell of diesel into the room from the street below. She was back in Paris.

In the quaint room her Aunt Edith so generously let her call home for a time, she threw open the old oak wardrobe to smells of lavender and musk. While she stood, barefoot and confused, wearing nothing but a large, white muslin Henley, she stared at the mostly empty wardrobe contents. Inside was a long white embroidered blouse that she had always coveted of her sister Anna's. Rose touched the fabric, dismayed at her perceived kleptomania.

Now wide-awake and home in Paris, she was glad the nightmare of the past week was over. Longing for family and the familiar tugged at her with a bittersweet pull. She had traveled from Rome the night before. It was all coming back to her. She dressed, tying a silk wraparound skirt around her waist, tugged on her Frye boots, and stepped quietly through the apartment. She wanted to see who was home in this eerily quiet day. She found Aunt Edith in the kitchen making soup for lunch.

"Bonjour, sleepyhead."

Rose pushed messy hair from her face. "What time is it?"

"*Il est neuf heure!* I let you sleep. You got back so late."

"*Merci.* What's going on?" Rose glanced around the empty apartment.

Edith ushered Rose into the dining room. She poured warm milk into a large mug and broke all rules by joining her for *Café au lait* at such a late hour.

"How was Rome?" Aunt Edith perched at the edge of the seat, her face open and curious.

"It's a great, beautiful, crowded city!" Rose smiled at her kind Aunt, who seldom if ever sat still.

"Oopf! With crazy drivers. Not as beautiful as Paris."

"Of course not," Rose laughed. "Short trip though. I forgot my Youth Hostel card so it was hard to find a cheap Hotel. I ended up staying with Nuns up on Vatican Hill. That is a huge place. I was in St. Peters Square when the white smoke came from the Sistine chapel."

"Momentous occasion." Edith nodded solemnly. Rose's uncle Edith's favorite American cousin, Rene, now Father Thomas, was a catholic priest,

Rose placed one square of brown sugar cube in the cup with silver tongs. Everything here was old world. The solid wood dining table was large enough for twelve. It filled the entire room. A bay window at the end of the room held a deep love seat and two comfortable armchairs. She stirred the coffee around with a silver spoon watching the swirl of cream in dark roast coffee. Each pleasure, that much richer, after roughing it for four long days into nights in Italy.

Rose had slept through breakfast, and dinner would be served promptly at noon. She was more curious than hungry. Edith was looking at her intently.

"Your sister Anna came."

"What? You're kidding? I saw her shirt in the wardrobe. I thought I was still dreaming."

"She came here from America to visit you. She said it's her summer break before school starts."

"Where is she? Has she gone out? Shopping or something?" Rose smiled when she heard Aunt Edith's news. Inside she trembled. The real question was why? Why had her sister traveled all the way from Texas?

"She left for Italy yesterday. In the morning."

"What?" Rose's spoon clattered to the table.

"You were in Italy. I told her, so she left. I didn't expect you back so soon. Or rather, late last night."

Rose wiped up her mess with an embroidered napkin. "How?"

"By train. She went to the station." She shrugged apologetically, "We didn't know when you would be back."

"I must go back to Italy right away to find her." She half jumped up from the table. "Does she have a Eurrail pass?"

"I don't think so."

"I do. I'm still packed." Rose quickly swallowed the coffee. "I'll just freshen up and go."

"Brush your hair. Your grandmother will never forgive me. It's bad enough you don't wear a slip with those skirts of yours." Edith finished her coffee. "How will you find her?"

Rose couldn't explain to her Aunt that, as sisters, they had fully functioning intuition. They only had to think the thought and the phone would ring or whatever. They didn't talk about it, they just did it.

"I will leave signs. I will post them everywhere. Which town did she go to?"

"Florence. She said she would go to Florence."

In those days, 1977, everyone traveled around Europe with backpacks and Eurrail passes and stayed in Youth Hostels on the cheap. "That's right. That was my plan. I'll find her."

Back in her room—correction, the spare bedroom/library Aunt Edith had so generously let her call home for the year of her long visit—Rose stared at the telltale signs of Anna's presence. Anna had been here while Rose was still gone on her travels exploring Europe. Rose hadn't known she was coming. She had wished she would come and had certainly invited her in many letters home. Rose was shocked by the surprise, except, now that she was here, Anna had left. Taken off in the spontaneous, or impatient way, all of the girls in their family had. What did she want? It must be urgent or she wouldn't have chased her to Italy.

Rose planned to immerse herself in the French culture. She wanted above all to fit in with her French family. She'd left University mid-semester to earn enough money for the trip. She should go back and finish college, but she wanted to stay here, and develop her art at an Atelier. Or the Beaux's Arts if that were possible. If only...

Rose was determined to stay. Her grandmother had married an American and moved to America. Now she could reverse that if she could meet a French man. If she had been lucky enough to be born here in Paris, she would already know the language. But no. Now she was afflicted with being an American. All over Europe, wherever Rose traveled, they had made fun of her for being so ignorant and naïve about the world, politics, and socialism. Americans were not respected as far as those around here she'd met. Paris, to her, felt like the center of the universe. Paris was the most amazing city she had ever seen. It was a marvel of Design and engineering.

Designed by the famous city planner, Georges-Eugène, or 'Baron' Haussmann, Paris fanned out like the spokes of a wheel. Monuments placed at the hubs worked as central foci. This way she could head off down quaint sides streets lined by small shops and stay oriented by the monument at Place du Concord. Then embark down another and find the Jardin des Tuileries. Arches and monuments punctuated the city. The buildings all matched, a solid six stories in every direction with the uniform mansard roofs at the top floor. She loved how she could see Sacré-Cœur crowning Montmartre from almost any point in the city. It was so big.

She looked forward to dragging Anna up the million stone steps to that old part of Paris. The history of Toulouse-Lautrec and Picasso etched into the very cobblestones. Funny how the excitement tangled her emotions. Anna's presence here did not bode well. Why, oh why had she come?

Rose hoped there wasn't a disaster on the home front. Her whole life hung upon a thread of possibility. As excited as Rose was to see her sister, thoughts of her family filled her with dread. She had been gone a long time by now. And she'd tasted freedom. Her younger sister Anna—the three of them, Anna, Murielle and she—ran things at home. But that life was far away now, like a forgotten time. Anna was only seventeen, and still in High School. Rose had a couple of years of University under her belt. It can be lonely running all over Europe alone at times. Her heart soared at the prospect of finding Anna.

Rose always wanted to see Michelangelo's David. Anna knew that about her. She talked about David constantly. She was devoted to Michelangelo, and King David, and the young David. If David was alive today, she would marry him. She would head to Florence now, determined that they would find each other. Surely her fears were unfounded.

The apartment on *Rue des Londres* was not far from Gare St. Lazare. The train station and Rose were becoming great friends. She kissed Edith on both cheeks before she dashed out of the apartment. Her pack fully loaded with essentials and sketchbooks, bounced as she tore down the three flights of stairs. Her hand slid along the polished wood banister as she spiraled down the land-ing, the musty smells fragrant to her now, in her home away from home.

Having the Eurrail pass made trips around the conti-nent a no brainer. She searched the ticket window for times of trains to Florence or Rome. Summertime made it easy to travel. Jeans, white shirts, a few wraparound skirts, pencils, as well as journals for writing and sketching, and she was equipped.

Rose stood on the platform watching people charge off the train before she could board. And there was Anna. Right there standing out from the crowd here in Paris. She couldn't believe her eyes. Anna, disembarking and saun-tering along the platform.

"Anna!" she cried.

Anna smiled a huge smile when she saw her.

"I was headed to Italy to find you!"

"I came back! I stayed on the train as I thought it just

might be smarter to find you in Paris. As, I know where you live."

Rose's heart leapt at the joy of seeing her sister. Anna walked straight out of the past she'd left and into her present teetering on tall wedges, a large red duffel packed to the gills, thrown over her shoulder. Her auburn hair shone in the sunlight.

"I can't believe my eyes. You came all this way to visit me. Shall we go back to our Aunt Edith's place?"

Anna linked her arm through Rose's. "Let's head to one of those Parisian café's sister. We need to talk."

Once seated at a table in a small café, sipping a café au lait, Rose asked, "Tell me Anna, what brings you to Paris?" Her heart raced as she kept her tone casual.

Anna caught her up on the latest dramas and disasters that catching up on the home front entailed. She laughed it all off with a forced bravado.

"You mean there is nothing wrong? No big problem?" Rose asked.

"I needed a break, sister." It was clear neither of them left to find adventure, as much as to experience peace and normalcy on foreign territory. By the time Anna finished a few tales, Rose was very glad to be living in Paris and not back at home.

"Wait," she sobered up after laughing uncontrollably at the last story. "We have to make it back in time for tea so Aunt Edith knows to expect us both for dinner."

"You're right, there is a reason I came. I want you to come back home," Anna said. "Edith thinks we are both gone. We will be an imposition if we show up now."

"Nonsense, she will be glad to see us. Both. And together." After a pause, "I will," Rose answered Anna's concern. "It's just a trip."

"You might forget about us. What time is tea?"

"Five. Dinner is promptly at eight." Rose's mind swirled in a tangle of thoughts she couldn't explain to one so young. "There is order and certainty here. I love that."

"Just call her. I am used to more freedom, besides, this is our chance to explore Paris together."

2
THE CHURCH OF ST. GENEVIEVE

*R*ose grabbed Anna's hand and led her through small streets, past shop windows, and cut through an arcade. Rose had a big city stride in her Frye boots. Anna tottered along in her tall wedge sandals. Rose called Edith from a payphone and explained that she and Anna were in Paris together, and she would show her some sights before returning in time for dinner. "I want to show her the church of St. Geneviève that Gramma Yvonne was married in. It's not far from here."

"Diner is at eight. Don't be late, Rose. Jean Françoise will be joining us tonight."

Rose giggled a bit when she hung up the phone. She explained that Jean François was her absolute favorite third cousin.

"Wait until you meet him, he speaks English and everything." She grabbed Anna's hand to wind their way through the streets to the Church of St. Genevieve.

Nothing is as it seems. Her sister looked like a normal teen. But Rose knew that nature had designed her as a solid stocky aggressive basketball player. Now the wind could blow her over.

"Wait. Slow down. It's fine. I'm so happy to be here with you. This is my first time to walk these neighbor-hoods. I'm enjoying the walk—the streets—the shops. Look at that." She pointed at a window full of elegant women's shoes and purses. "I didn't go out alone much on the first few days after I got here."

"This Church is amazing; wait till you see it. It's one of the oldest in Paris. Gramma Yvonne and Jean Claude were married there. Gramma always said it was love at first sight for her."

"That old bag? In love? Hard to picture it."

"People aren't born old." God she's rude. "You don't know her like I do."

Anna pulled her into a cheese shop.

"*Bounjour,*" the bell tinkled as they opened the door.

"*Bonjour.*" They surveyed the choices and bought blue cheese and some English cheddar. Then they dashed across the street to a fruit stand and bought a few red apples. As they crossed the Seine on one of the old bridges, Rose spotted a small park tucked back from the street. The two plopped down on a green painted park bench and put down their packs.

Rose pulled a pocketknife from her pack and sliced the apples. The white wrapper the cheese came in became an impromptu plate. "A picnic, of sorts. I haven't had a chance to eat today. Actually I'm getting jittery on all this coffee."

"Coffee is great. Energy without all the calories."

Rose's eyes widened. "When I am traveling, I usually make do on cheese, baguettes and fruit. When I live with Edith and Jean, it's a full three gourmet meals a day. But my stomach shrunk on the last trip because I ran low on traveler's checks and tried to stretch my few dollars. Aunt Edith never eats in restaurants when we are in Paris, so I have no idea how to order, or what to eat. Besides, picnicking seems to fit my budget."

"It's fine with me too." Anna was already on her third apple, and ate it all the way to the core. Slicing was a bit too civilized for her. "Aunt Edith doesn't like me too much, I think."

"Sure she does. We're family. You don't speak French. It's hard on them."

Anna changed the subject with a few anecdotes about their little sisters as they continued their journey. Soon Rose spotted the worn wood door with a curved arch top that was left ajar with a rusted metal lock beyond repair. She led her through the stone wall into a small courtyard at the side of the church. "Here she is," she announced. She touched the 500-year-old stone of the church wall.

"Is this the back entrance?"

Rose shrugged. She loved old courtyards. Tangled vines with white flowering jasmine wound around the wall like a coiled rope. They walked around to the front of the church and tried the door. They pushed it open to the quiet dim interior. The sounds of the street were muffled once they were within. Rose walked reverently down the aisle and slipped in to kneel and say a few prayers.

Anna pranced straight up the aisle to the altar. She strutted as though on a runway. Once she reached the altar she tossed her head and made a spin. She lowered her head and stared straight at Rose, then flipped her hair over her shoulder and sauntered back down. Her heels clicked sharply on the stone, echoing through the empty church.

"I've been at modeling school. I am practicing runway

now. That's my goal. I'm going to be a top runway model. That's how I will change my destiny. I will be a totally independent woman."

"Anna, this is a church."

She shrugged and grinned.

Rose knelt in the pew and studied the ornate alter. Her head arched back to study the complicated stained glass windows that formed tall gothic arches. The oil paintings were huge and dark with age. She contemplated time. The blink of an eye between when her grandmother wed in December 1919, and now, 1977, with two sisters in Paris, complete opposites.

"This is a great place to practice. This city is so crowded and packed with people." Anna pranced up the aisle and back, each footfall echoing and stirring up musky frankincense into the air.

Rose glanced at her watch. "Anna hurry, we've got to get back to Aunt Edith's. She'll kill me if I'm late." Rose shrugged her pack back on her sweaty back. "Jean Françoise is her oldest and favorite son. I know a short cut."

Anna grabbed her duffel, taking the time to smooth her hair.

Rose realized it was slower going with luggage and heels. "She hates it when I'm late." Why had Anna come? The thought still nagged. And how had she paid for the trip?

THEY BURST INTO THE APARTMENT, THEIR VOICES TOO loud, Rose realized, as they entered the hushed hallway. Luckily everyone was gathered by the bay window and were still visiting, milling around the table in animated conversation. The solid oak table gleamed with silver place settings and white linen napkins. When she spotted Jean Françoise Rose realized, he must be at least 31 or 32 by now. She had only been eleven when she'd had her first crush on him. Distracted by his charming grin she put her concerns away.

3
DINNER

*A*unt Edith made the introductions. Everyone greeted them with kisses on both cheeks.

"Stephan, you remember cousin Anna? Jean Françoise, this is Rose's sister Anna."

"How are you?" he said in gently accented English.

Anna stared tongue tied and shy. All the runway bravado had taken a back seat in this new setting.

Everyone spoke ninety miles an hour in French. Rose shrugged at Anna and the two found their places when everyone else resumed their normal seats. Uncle Jean faced Edith at the head of the table. She saddled soup from the tureen into bowls and passed them around. Rose remembered her childhood visit to Paris when Gramma Yvonne and she had stayed with Uncle Rene, Edith s father. His cook served each person's soup for the first course and would appear later to remove the bowls and pass out clean plates. Edith followed the same system, but the clean plate was beneath the soup bowl. As everyone *"oo'd and -ah -la-la'd"* around her, Rose listened. As the French are quite expressive, gesticulating with hands, she could follow the essence of the conversation. Every now and then Stephan or Jean Françoise would clue her in on the topic in English. She knew she should speak French better by now. Instead she studied the candlelight reflected on the silver service before her. The two forks on the left, two spoons, one for soup one for coffee on the right, the knife and a little silver bridge the utensils should rest on so as not to soil the white tablecloth. Rose slid her napkin out of the silver ring with Yvonne's initials on it. It touched her that a place awaited her Gramma always, even though her visits were few and far over the years. Her presence made Yvonne closer she supposed. Everyone had their initials engraved on the silver napkin rings. It struck her that this ritual of dining with silver and white tablecloths was like the Catholic Mass with golden chalices and pressed linens. Anna was wiggling in her chair, like she longed for escape.

Rose dipped her soupspoon into the cold vichyssoise she had never tasted until she had come here—and craved while on her travels. Lately she had been subsisting on sardines, cheeses, and baguettes from local shops.

Dinnertime was a big feast in her opinion. The main course was spinach mushroom quiche served with the thinnest homemade *pomme frites*. She ate each bite, savoring it, chewing slowly. There was a lull in the conversation and Rose looked up, everyone was staring at her. After she swallowed her last bite the next course was served. Such were the French table manners; all were served the new course at the same time. They had all waited patiently while she savored each morsel. Edith passed out bowls of salad and they passed them around the table till everyone was served.

All were excited about Jean Françoise's latest job on a film set. He'd been gone most of the summer on a shoot. Some slightly known American Actor was in it, she surmised, as they said his name often, alternating with expressions of disbelief or disgust.

For the final desert course, Edith placed a platter of cheeses on the table. Stephan passed around clean plates. Everyone sampled a slice of the various offerings. Rose noticed Anna had passed up the baguette when it was handed around. Edith urged her to have at least a slice. "Ugh," she grumbled when Anna refused and instead, took a large serving of camembert cheese. Anna did have odd eating habits. She'd eaten the quiche right out of the crust. Edith had grumbled at that too. No one wasted anything here.

Jean Françoise was a freelance film editor, but he was involved in various aspects of the business. Rose watched and listened and pieced things together the best she could, as was her habit. She thought it would be nice to draw his portrait. The candles lit his face accentuating a strong jaw line. His auburn curls shone on his shirt collar. She was too much of a dreamer to even need to follow everything that was said. As she watched Anna, Rose knew she was bored to tears.

Edith collected all of the used plates into a pile and each was placed on the kitchen cart beside the dining table. After dinner the group crowded into the kitchen as was the daily custom. Edith donned long rubber gloves and filled the sink with steaming soapy water. She proceeded to wash each dish by hand with gusto and the seven, each with a crisp white dishtowel, dried and placed each dish in stacks according to size. Edith washed the entire group of silver last and each piece shone as everyone dried and polished at once. Edith turned to Rose, "Always remember, the French wife is the queen of her kitchen."

Jean laughed as the group trouped back out to the living room with the dish cart full of clean dishes in the lead, like a train. Jean Gallaud, Edith's husband, an interior designer who had designed all the furniture and had it custom made, would entertain everyone with antics. Anna finally laughed when Jean said, "choo-choo" as he pushed the cart to the large wood hutch where all of the dishes and linens were stored.

"Pay no attention. The French wife...Pooh. Times have changed, the modern French woman is quite different." Jean Francois waved his Mothers comments away.

"It's true," Aunt Edith insisted.

After Jean Francois left, Anna asked Rose if she could take a bath. Rose helped her get situated with a bar of olive oil soap and fresh towels. After she closed the door and joined Edith and Jean in the sitting room, Edith looked extremely nervous. Jean Françoise had counseled Rose to be careful as his mother tended to get uptight and nervous if anything was out of order or routine. Edith was clearly agitated, doing her embroidery with a vengeance, and muttering to Jean.

"What is it?" Rose asked.

"Don't let your sister fill the water too high in the tub. She is so-o big, this is an old apartment."

She laughed, "What? Why?"

Edith shrugged and lifted her eyebrows her face serious. "She could fall through the floor."

Rose realized that Anna's height was intimidating to these petite French around her. She obediently relayed the message.

"You have got to be kidding!"

"Just be sparing OK?"

"Okay. Okay."

When she reassured Edith the bath water was under control. She replied, "The tomato is missing."

"Huh?"

"For tomorrows salad. She took the tomato."

After a few more days of walking on eggshells, Rose knew she didn't want to wear out her welcome. She realized Edith and Jean were fine with one American cousin, but two guests were just too much. No wonder Anna had left to find her rather than stay here alone.

DESPITE THE AWKWARD VIBES, THE SISTERS HAD A LOT OF fun that week. After shopping for fabric at the market, Rose designed outfits for Anna to wear. She wore clothes well, and it was fun to do. Rose understood why the fashion world needed models to display the clothes to the best advantage. She designed and sewed a sort of two-tone dinner jacket. A deep teal blue silk for the collar and cuffs, with the body tailored from a rich paisley brocade. The sash she made, matched the cuffs. Rose had designed some camisole style tank tops that Anna admired of hers. She used macramé with stones and seashells woven into the straps. One shirt laced up the back. It was good for summer and beaches. Rose, as the oldest, had noticed that behavior with her sisters before. If it was hers, they wanted it. Her sister Murielle never wanted to borrow *any* old shirt, she wanted her *favorite* shirt. It would be lucky if she ever saw it again. Anna told her funny stories about Murielle using Rose's birth certificate to get in to nightclubs. She used her name as well, passing herself off as Rose. They didn't look that much alike. Rose cringed to think what trouble she might get into in Houston while she wasn't even around.

"Edith watches me like a hawk. They're like the police."

"Anna, this is their home. It's a lot to feed us and make sure we are home on time etcetera. I try hard to fit in here, they have their system."

"Yeah and you love it."

"I do. I admit it. They don't waste anything here. If it's a cool day, you grab a sweater. You don't crank up the heat. She even gives the cheese rinds to the birds at the kitchen window. She angles the French windows to catch the breezes and ceiling fans keep everything cool. The meals are like a ritual. I do love that."

Rose favorite time was the after lunch coffee. Edith had a chemist's test tube that she placed over a Bunsen burner at the table. The coffee beans were mixed to her own special blend, once ground they were placed in the top compartment. The flame created a percolated coffee that would boil thru and then drip back down into the tube. After it was done she blew out the flame and served the coffee in small espresso cups. The ritual was wrapped in the fragrant aroma of roasted coffee. Edith grabbed the tin of dark chocolates and passed them around. As Rose dipped the tip of one of the dark squares in the coffee, it was perfection.

Later back in the room they shared, sitting on the bed, Rose poked through Anna's luggage, exploring her camera lenses. "I love Paris too. I have been all over. There is a lot I can show you."

"Let's travel together."

"You don't have a Eurrail pass. And it doesn't make sense to get one if you will only be here one month."

"I couldn't afford it. You have already been to a lot of countries. Have you ever explored France?"

Rose took a few candid shots of Anna while they plotted their trip.

"We should go to the Riviera," Anna decided. "It's on the coast and it's famous. That's where the scene is. We need to hit the scene."

"Anna, how did you afford to come all the way to Paris?"

"I saved up the money I made at the restaurant and bought a ticket. It's a round-trip special they ran on Air France. I knew I could stay with you."

"Yeah." And Rose was stretching a small bit of carefully saved cash over nine months. The further it stretched the longer she could stay. She thought. *I don't want to go back ever.*

Rose studied Anna through the lens, her long body and her slender neck. She looked pretty when she was enthused. This seventeen-year-old young woman had transformed herself from the solidly built aggressive basketball player she'd been at fifteen. She'd lost 30 pounds, had been to modeling school, and traveled to Paris to have an adventure with her. The world was out there, "What are we waiting for!" Rose said aloud. "Okay, you're on."

4

ON THE ROAD

*E*ventually, Edith and her son Stephan, a teacher, enthused by the prospect of their adventure, supplied them with maps. August was hot in Paris, but they would travel through the French Alps en route. Stephan advised them to pack light and for warmth as well. Edith lent Rose a prized wool army blanket.

Anna and Rose now had passports, traveler's checks, maps and a sketchy plan. On a bright, too-hot, August day, they left after breakfast taking the Paris Metro to the end of the line. Then, thumbs out, they hit the road. That was the way to travel in those days. Optimism prevailed, and the adventure began. They were on the road.

Rose was mesmerized by the lenses, equipment, and knowledge Anna had about cameras. That techie stuff didn't stick in her brain. She didn't even believe Photography was an art form. She believed in drawing and painting from models like in the Renaissance. That's why she was here in Europe, like a sponge, learning, absorbing everything.

"I've been working in Dad's darkroom most afternoons

this summer. My shift at the restaurant doesn't start until five. Dad needs the help and I love it."

"That's great!"

Now, with Paris far behind them, and the open road in front, they felt free. The two sisters strolled down the empty country road. The breeze blew up Rose's legs in her flowing calf-length skirt. While Anna strolled in huge bell-bottom hip huggers. They both glanced up at a huge sculpture placed on the edge of a quaint village. Rose ran up and climbed the iron horse by grasping the legs of a soldier. It was a group of horses and a warrior—larger than life, the bronze cold to the touch. While entertaining themselves posing and shooting pictures of each other, a yellow citron stopped. The driver offered to take a few photos of the two of them together. He was pleased with their American accents.

"Where are you headed?" Anna thought to ask.

"I'm headed south, towards the French Alps."

Rose and Anna looked at each other and grinned.

"We'd like to go there!"

"Hop in. I'll give you a ride."

As he drove, Henri explained much about the history of the area and the monument they had been so enamored with. He asked if they were thirsty and then stopped at a small town for a café. Rose sketched his portrait as a gift for the ride and the coffee. Having photo shoots until a ride shows up is a creative way to travel, she thought.

The countryside and small towns flew by in a whirl of rides and faces, young and old, and stories in French and thick accented English. The two lost track of towns, enjoying cheese shops and fruit stands along the way of their travels.

Anna caught Rose staring at sweet shops and bakeries. "That is pure poison," she announced. "The belly is a bread basket. That's were bread goes when you eat it. So said our Great Grandmother anyway."

"I know. 'One is only as young as the spine is supple.' " Rose loved that truism she had often heard as a kid. Taking it literally they entertained themselves with Yoga and spine stretches by the side of the road. They felt energized and lithe as dancers as they danced and kicked and breathed in the marvelous freedom of the open country roads.

5

BERNARD -ALPS

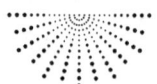

*T*hen came Bernard. He spotted them on a country road just outside the quaint, exquisite town of Chambéry. He was an accountant. After a day in the office, he headed to his home in Grenoble, on his way back from a meeting. When the girls explained that they wanted to see the French Alps, he took them all the way. The group wound around the exciting roads all the way to the snowy peaks.

"Snow yikes," Anna said. Summer in snowy mountain peaks was not what they had bargained for. When it was time to get out, and begin the hike, it was already getting late. As Texans they hadn't seen snow ever, and were not prepared. Anna smiled. Rose's hair whipped around her face as she got out and reached in and grabbed both packs with gusto from the back seat. She helped Anna adjust her bag like a pack to facilitate a good mountain hike. They smiled and waved *as if* they knew exactly what to do. Bernard said, "Cheerio." and drove off. Rose gave a tiny wave. They both stood shivering, frozen to the spot, staring at the tall peaks and windy rock strewn path. The wind wrapped itself around Anna's long legs and her toes were turning blue in her dainty sandals.

Then as they watched, Bernard abruptly stopped the car and backed up. He got out of the car and zipped up his down parka. "Look, I have an idea. I don't want to leave you up here this late. You can stay with me at my apartment and then I'll give you a ride out here in the morning and you can explore the mountains all you want. I have some warm sweaters and coats you can borrow or I'll take you into town to get more supplies. In the meantime, I know a cozy café, we'll get some hot chocolate and dinner later on if you're up for it."

Rose looked at Anna. Anna smiled a big smile. "That is a wonderful idea."

"Only if you are sure we are not imposing." Rose looked hopeful. Getting to know him better over hot chocolate was wonderful.

"Not at all. You too are a welcome addition to my predictable routine. In fact, I insist. I haven't been up here in a while and I enjoy the drive. I know a lovely bistro in a nearby town."

"What about your wife? Or family?" Rose asked.

"I live alone. Don't worry. I have a big place. Guest rooms and everything. I would have said something earlier but you seemed so sure of yourselves. And besides, you're American. Who knows?"

"You mean we might be crazy or something," Anna volunteered.

"Se Normal!"

The three drove in silence back down the mountain as the sun lowered in a spectacular show. They were headed into the valley with a quaint mountain town. Well someone in the group was sane, Rose thought. Spontaneous living is a good creative way to be, but neither sister had really planned on snow.

The three bonded right there and then, over their fool-hardy plan. As they laughed about the escapade over nice cups of hot chocolate, they relaxed and felt comfortable in Bernard's solid practicality. He was sincere in the offer of a place to stay at night and explore by day. In the end it was all decided.

The girls got to be great friends with Bernard as he was as good as his word. His flat in town was small and clean with an austere guest room. By day, Anna and Rose would head off on a tour of the area, but would always join Bernard back at his place for dinner. He went off to his office in the mornings and didn't question their chosen mode of transport; which was their thumbs. They were able to dress warm enough, and on the numerous mountain hikes, they explored gorges, splendid vistas, and hidden waterfalls.

Being based in town meant they stayed well supplied with film. Anna habitually sent the rolls back to their dad in America to be developed. She explained, Dad said, *I don't need a letter, just send your film back and I will have a visual story of your trip.* Their dad had been only one-year-old when his mom, their Gramma had taken him to France. He'd been with his mom and elder brother, Stephan. He hadn't remembered a thing. He'd never visited as an adult. Rose, on the other hand, couldn't wait to be an ex-patriot. She was embarrassed about American behavior as she traveled. So far she'd traveled alone and kept her mouth shut. Better to observe and later befriend fellow travelers There was much about America she detested. Suburban sprawl was a big one. And how the whole country had been developed around the car. In contrast, in Europe everything was based on pedestrians and mass transit.

Anna seemed to attract a different reaction. She called herself a Texan, that seemed to make the difference.

They spent three glorious days exploring country lanes and mountain vistas. Everyone they encountered posed for their traveling photo shoot. They took shots of each other with their new friends as they explored France. Finally, as preparation for the rest of the trip, Anna bought a few pounds of rice and cooked a big batch on Bernard's stove. Anna was on a severe diet. Rose could see it worked well on her, and was hungry enough to try anything. Anna was almost six feet tall in heels and she had Rose convinced she was runway material. As a result they weren't getting much exercise, but there was no problem getting rides. Apparently rice was on the approved food list.

As she stirred cups of rice into boiling water, Anna said, "Bernard is great."

"Yeah," Rose said, as she gazed around the room. She liked the narrow high ceilinged kitchen, pale yellow with a big gas stove. A traditional red checked tablecloth covered the wood table.

Bernard had a selection of pots and pans hanging from a pot rack, but as a bachelor, didn't have near the equipment Edith had crammed into her kitchen. She could make everything from homemade French fries sliced thin, to farmer's cheese and fresh whipped cream.

"You know what I'm thinking."

"Time to move on."

"Yeah, I don't want to wear out our welcome."

"I am grateful and all, but I really wanted to spend the night in a barn or something."

"Like real runaways."

"You mean like Nancy and Plum in the story?"

"Right. Just like Nancy and Plum. It's awful having such nice understanding parents. We can't even run away to Europe because they gave us their blessing and told us to send photos. We had no reason to run away when we were young," Rose whined. "I know, if they were the beating kind, I would have been out of there like a shot. I was just poised, back pack already loaded."

"You did run away when you were thirteen. I remember that now." Anna said.

"Well, it was really for the adventure. This guy named Jimmy said he would hop a train. That sounded like a cool adventure. I used to like Jimmy too. My new boyfriend John planned to go with him. I knew I would miss him if he left. It sounded so final. Of course John did have a terrible family life so he had a reason. "

"Ooh tell me the story," Anna said.

"OK. Well, Jimmy, John, and Bobby wanted to tag along too. John wanted me to come. I snuck out of the house through a window in my bedroom. It was the middle of the night. We went to the field to wait for the train. It took forever. It was almost dawn when we finally heard the train. And when it came, it went so fast. It sped right by. We were all too chicken to get on.

"We slept in the fields then. Later we were hungry so we walked into a grocery store and got a bunch of food and supplies. I got toothbrushes for everyone. It turned out some of the boys had never seen a toothbrush. It's funny. Once I had officially left home, I couldn't go back. We stayed gone for two and a half days. When the neighbors found me, they were a bit upset."

"Gabrielle woke up Mom and said you were missing. Mom didn't even believe her. It's when she found herself searching the refrigerator, that she realized you were truly gone. They didn't call the police. They just told the neighbors and everyone went out searching."

"I remember when Mr. Dillinger showed up looking all

self-righteous. I said, 'Hey, Mr. Dillinger, what are you doing here?' 'Looking for you, he said.' I was in pretty big trouble. After that Mom said I should have a party at my house every weekend so my friends could come over. So I did. They were glad to get off the streets and have a place to go.

"The biggest problem for me came a few days later. It turns out Bobby had a big fan club entirely made up of thirteen year-olds. One afternoon I was minding my own business, walking home from school by myself, I heard someone shouting curse words at me. Next think you know, a pack of teen girls chased me down the street with threats, shaking sticks at me. They accused me of running away with their boyfriend, Bobby. I didn't like Bobby. He was a freckled face pipsqueak. It was so scary being chased by a pack of irate teen girls. They clutched sticks in their fists with chipped pink nail polish. One girl, Darlene, was foaming at the mouth, her eyes slit like foxes. I stayed home for a couple of weeks after that.

"No one to beat us or misunderstand us at home," mused Rose. "I think it's because our parents are both philosophy majors. And Dad was almost a priest. That's almost like being a communist. All about communal living and the good of the people."

"Our life in America has been too easy, too middle class." Anna agreed.

"After I read '*Siddhartha*' I really wanted to wander the earth with few possessions and rely on the kindness of strangers," Rose said.

"Right. I think the *kindness of strangers* thing comes from Blanche Dubois." Anna rolled her eyes.

"I like that name."

"Come on, '*Streetcar Named Desire?*' You're the one who went to college. I'll make another batch of rice for our trip. We can pack it into these mason jars and carry it with us."

"Good idea." Rose smile was dreamy, at the memory of her spunky, thirteen-year-old, self.

The girls called it rice pudding when they added honey they bought at a small shop, and that became their staple. When he heard their plan, Bernard generously offered to give them a ride out of town as a head start on their new journey. After teary good byes and exchange of addresses so they could send him some photos, Anna and Rose were on their own again. Once outside of some small town they had a rather long stretch with few cars. Then they hit the jackpot after a few miles when they stumbled upon an apple orchard full of small green apples.

6

APPLE ORCHARD

| 'In the woods'

*A*nna and Rose, exhausted, plopped down on a large white boulder. Rose's eyes and senses were filled with the natural beauty of these fields and orchards. They had left the road and meandered, across the lush meadows, as there were so few cars this time of day. Rose selected one of the apples and carefully sliced the tart fruit into small pieces.

Anna mixed it into the rice. "We can eat this for three days if we ration it."

As they wandered through the orchard, Rose spotted a stone farmhouse in the distance. "Let's head that way and check it out."

When they arrived at the small dwelling, Rose knocked at the door.

When the door opened, Rose blurted, "I noticed you have a barn out back." Rose spoke quickly before she could loose her nerve. "My sister and I are traveling through the area and we wondered if we could spend the night in it?"

The farmer, a balding middle-aged man in a white t-shirt, shrugged. His wife, a small woman in an apron peered out from behind him. With a mixture of choppy French and big arm gestures, Rose explained their plight traveling through, and needing a place to rest for the night. She pointed to the barn and gestured a lot because her French was terrible and this was the first person she'd encountered who couldn't speak English. After listening with a patient weariness, the farm wife got the picture. She said something like Anna was so pretty —*très jolie* and she insisted on providing them with a pile of blankets and pillows. Anna and Rose thanked them profusely.

Once settled in the sweet, hay-smelling barn, they were both exhausted. After another repast of rice and apples, they made a nest with piles of hay and blankets. Once ensconced and cozy, Rose found herself wide-awake, staring up at the stars through pinholes in the thatched roof.

"You know our parents don't know where we are," Rose stated.

"They think they do. They think we are at Aunt Edith's in Paris. That's where our mail comes."

"They are too busy to know, or wonder, or care where we are."

"Yep."

"They have their hands full," Rose said.

"Mom with all the kids—Rene, Margaret, Katarina, Lily, Rob, and Thomas.

"Lots of mouths to feed."

"Why do you think I had to get away?" Anna's voice was strained.

"Yes. Like me, we both had to get away."

"Peace and quiet on a starry night."

"It's like camping."

"Dad always took us camping."

"God. I used to cook dinner almost every night," Rose said.

"Except when you went to Dad's house. So who do you think does it now?" Anna's brown eyes penetrated her.

"Not Murielle."

"Right. Does she even know how to cook?"

"Wow, Anna. I'm so sorry." Rose was filled with dismay. "Since I have been gone to college—that's about three years now—I have left you with it all." Rose felt so selfish. She had been so impatient, focused on getting to college to get a degree and embark on a new life. She hadn't thought about all of the sisters she'd abandoned in her haste. "Surely, Rene pitches in?"

"Hah! Yeah." Anna stared off. "I love helping Dad in the darkroom. It's quiet in the dark room."

"You graduate this year." Rose suddenly thought about Rene, only fourteen. She was the oldest of the little kids. "Where are you gonna go to college?"

"I want to study commercial art; graphic design and

interior design. You know? Make money being artistic. I have no interest in being a starving artist." Anna adjusted herself in the blankets. "That's the back-up plan. You know, the modeling."

Rose hid her surprise. Many in her family were talented at art or dance. She hadn't realized Anna had such drive. "You are pretty good at starving as a model," she quipped.

"Face it. I'm going to be rich. Somehow."

Rose did believe that. "You are right. You always won at monopoly."

"My real dream is to be a runway model. I used my waitressing money to go to modeling school." Anna's voice was more determined than enthused.

"I like your hair cut. Very vogue." Rose knew persistence was the big half of the battle.

Anna tossed her head and ran her fingers through her sun streaked shaggy bangs. Rose noticed how that cut framed Anna's large almond eyes, dark chocolate brown. They could make your heart melt when she was sad. Yet, when she laughed, Rose never quite saw it in her eyes. Perhaps she was always holding something in reserve. Rose realized she could seldom read her sister's thoughts. Perhaps this trip would bring them closer. "Penny for your thoughts?"

"I want Mom and Dad to get back together."

This was out of the blue. Rose wanted to keep the mood light. "What about his girl friends?"

"Sphuff. They are just hangers on, and wannabe's. They don't hold a candle to Mom, and you know that. Hell. He knows it." Anna turned to Rose, and touched her arm in the darkness. "He loves Mom. You know that."

"Yeah, he says so."

Rose realized Anna had been holding a lot inside. Yet all Rose had had to do was ask her.

"He talks about Mom all the time. He is home every weekend; cooking elaborate dinners, or bringing cool friends over to meet everyone."

"So he should be. Seriously, I'm glad to know he's still keeping that up."

"He is a great cook."

"Are you hungry?" Rose was sure she'd heard her stomach rumble.

"Hah. I must be, I am picturing that mouthwatering chicken, covered in spices and drenched in butter."

"And those Swedish meatballs floating in sour cream."

"He has French tastes."

"Cream and butter."

Both stomachs growled at the same time. Causing them both to fall into fits of laughter.

THE SUN STRIPED THE AIR WITH DUST MOTES THROUGH THE barn slats. It was morning. Rose opened her eyes slowly, as she could feel the sun on her lids. Anna was curled into a ball in the blankets in the hay. Rose sat up and could see the orchard beyond the square opening of the barn. Small apple trees stretched on and on covering the hill. Shaggy lime green grasses grew in tufts between the small trees. Anna rolled out of the soft cocoon and began picking hay out of her jeans. Rose got up and helped Anna fold the blankets. They piled them on a wood crate in the corner. A rooster called nearby. Rose felt great. She had blacked out somewhere in the middle of the conversation and slept sound.

"Alright Huckleberry Finn. Off we go."

'Apples in a tree'

Anna didn't say much, just smiled. She seemed happy, Rose thought. Talking and confiding last night had brought them closer somehow. Rose tore a sheet of paper from her journal. Right after the page she'd used to sketch the stonewall around the orchard, and a gnarled trunk with a bright green cap of leaves with mellow yellow-green apples. She penned a note addressed to the generous couple who'd shared their barn. She paired it with a quick small sketch and left it with the bedding.

As the sisters made their way slowly up hill, Anna gathered apples. Mostly they gleaned them from the ground. When a green-gold perfect round ball of an apple caught her eye, the sun making the leaves shine silver as it hung from the bough, Rose pulled it off. The apple felt good in her hand. After storing away ten or so while she walked, she finally took a bite. It was a good breakfast.

Neither girl spoke as they headed in the direction of the main road. The trek through the orchard and meadow was quite beautiful. There were tiny white star shaped flowers mixed in with the grasses. It may seem odd if she were to tell anyone they had happily slept in a barn and left before anyone could spot them, she mused. At home she'd slept on the floor all the time anyway. A palette on the floor was her norm. Here in Paris, at Aunt Edith's, she had her own bed all to herself. That was a luxury. When she lived at home, she awoke every morning to find her siblings, two or three of them sometimes, tucked into bed with her.

She'd never eaten so much in her life either. Three meals a day were customary at Edith's house. As she enjoyed the lush meadow, she knew she would never come this way again. She had no idea actually where they were. Just where they were headed. Headed for the South of France—The Riviera and the beaches. Aunt Edith had mentioned the castles along the Rhone were nice. They might pass some along the way.

7

CARCASSONNE- NICE

Sure enough, their next ride dropped them at Carcassonne. It was ten in the morning when they arrived. There were plenty of tourists milling about. They toured the castle and towers and moats and the keep.

| 'Carcassonne Castle'

Rose pulled out her sketchbook and began to draw a view of the castle from her perch on the wall. The rough stone pricked her bare legs where she sat. She drew another meticulous pencil sketch. Several hours had flown, by the time she was finished. For Rose, the focus was a kind of meditation.

Meanwhile, Anna explored on her own with her camera. They immersed themselves all day at the castle. Rose found the severe Romanesque mass of high stone walls that composed the castle were clean and almost modern. They made a picnic, sharing the last of the rice with lots of cut up apples. It was almost a meal. Reluctant to leave, they went to a nearby town and found a pension to spend the night. Anna relished a good shower before bed. They both were renewed after a good rest and ready for a fresh start the next morning.

ON THE ROAD AGAIN, BOTH GOT THEIR MORNING HIKE IN. Rose breathed in the crisp country air. She loved the exhilaration and freedom it gave her to walk along the highway on the way to somewhere. Whether she walked step by step, or someone gave her a lift, no matter, either way they would get there eventually. It was a game of chance. Would someone stop soon? Who would it be? How long would they walk? They only had to turn and walk backwards when they heard a car come by.

A few hours later, her feet were starting to blister. At least she had talked Anna into wearing some flat shoes for a change. She couldn't explain it. She felt happy and exhilarated. She called it *LIFE*. "I am human and fully alive in this moment. Everything I own is in this back pack," she announced to the world. Luckily it's an Army surplus, green canvas, heavy duty one.

Sunshine that warmed her face, and got in her eyes, shone upon her like life. She couldn't see anything but light. The sun shone with an intensity here stronger than in Texas She was full of light. And Life. She tried to hold the moment in her heart. Fullness to bursting—Joy. Such a small word for such a big feeling. Her smile was always too big for her face when she couldn't contain it in her heart any longer.

She heard the whir of a car in the distance. Smiling she turned around and extended her arm, her thumb poised to hitch. The car passed, and slowed, and then stopped and backed up. The two went to the car window.

"Where are you headed?"

"We're going to Nice."

"So are we."

"Hop in."

Anna looked at Rose with a knowing look. As if to say, Of course they were, We've enjoyed a wonderful day and now the adventure continues.

Arriving in Nice in a flurry of excitement, and kisses, and goodbyes—thanks for everything—the girls waved big arm waves, as the car spun around the large circle drive at the Hotel, and was gone. Now they had arrived, and everything was awkward.

THIS WAS A BIG TOWN. NOT AT ALL THE SAME AS THE BACK roads and villages they had been gleefully skipping through. As they entered through the revolving glass doors of the hotel into the grand two story marble lobby, they found themselves in a busy bustling sophisticated world of palm fronds and perfumed air. The sisters beelined to the ladies' room to clean up.

In the largest marble bathroom either had ever seen, there sat a small woman selling tiny pieces of brown toilet paper for a centime. They washed their hands and faces and rearranged their outfits into new looks. Rose's silky skirts never wrinkled. That's what was great about silk for travel. She put on a long black one, slender strapy sandals, used the large leather belt with the silver buckle to cinch her waist, and checked the mirror. She removed her white peasant blouse and layered a black tank with a royal blue paisley scarf. Anna put on cleanish jeans and got back into her heels. Large sunglasses gave her a glamorous look.

Rose knew above all not to look like a gypsy. She was going for sleek and demure and minimal. Gypsies were not all that welcome in Europe. When her grandmother called her one it was meant as a high insult. At first she'd always taken it as a complement. She secretly believed her Great Grandmother on her mother's side was a gypsy— fortuneteller. She was full of portents and healing reme- dies, the whole nine. Rose studied her own face in the gilt- edge mirror. She smoothed her curls down. She never wore make up so that wasn't an option.

The sisters chatted merrily and laughed as they exited the rest room and strode through the grand lobby and out into the intense sunshine, so noteworthy in the south of France. Intense sunlight reflected and bounced off every surface. She never wore sunglasses. She couldn't stand not to see clearly. She loved sun, and cobalt blue sky, with nothing to alter her vision or the color. However, she was a bit self-conscious, as she drug around her army-green, beat up backpack.

"How can I pretend this is the latest fashion state- ment?" she asked Anna as they sat down on a wrought iron park bench to plan their next move.

Busses of travelers pulled up in droves, emptying loads of tourists from every country imaginable for the Grand Hotel. Anna got up, tossed the bag over one shoulder, strutted a few paces and did a turn. She paused, looked over her shoulder with a straight face, then plopped back down. She took great care to hand the precious accessory back to Rose. If you own it, flaunt it. Rose got the message.

Both were struck dumb, as they took in the sight of the six hotels visible from their spot on the promenade. There was a wide boardwalk; endless white sand tumbled towards the bright blue sea. Deck chairs and striped umbrellas lined the beach. Waiters in white jackets held trays as they approached various groups around the beach. The whole affair looked like a very expensive party. Women in heels and big hats pushed suitcases on wheels, tipping porters as they swayed passed. Doormen, porters, and policemen, and a virtual army of uniformed servants bustled everywhere. Americans in Paris were somewhat anonymous. There seemed to be two classes at the Riviera. Rose's mind whirled around and around. She'd spent summer after summer in Santa Monica, but the beach was full of hippies gathered in groups strumming Beach Boys' songs on guitars; or athletes playing sand volleyball in baggy boxer bathing suits or cutoffs. When she'd trained as an actress, she'd always done improvisation. See the situation; adopt a role to deal with it; play the role. What were their options at seventeen and twenty? Did they look that young? They felt older than their years. But she was in way over her head. She knew it. Her French Gramma hated gypsies. That's why attire was so important to the French.

"How much money do we have? Can we get a room? Stay here? Now that we're here," Anna asked.

Rose did some quick calculations. Her rent at her garage apartment was $150 a month. Her life savings nest egg for college was $2,000. She only had a few hundred on her for the entire trip. It was a mini-miracle she had that. She'd been giving her Mom most of her earnings from her double summer jobs. She lived minimally while at college, by not owning a car and living in co-ops—communal living arrangements. She retained some of her earnings for her college expenses. With the open return airfare standby flight on sale, coupled with her French Aunts invitation to stay, she could afford this vacation. Sort of. The expenses at home were constant, like a black hole. She felt it her duty to contribute as much as she could, as the oldest. Funny, back home felt like a mirage, now that she was finally here. They were now, far from Paris. As she observed the scene she could see most people on the beach wore bathing suits.

"Our clothes won't matter so much out there." She wiped her sweaty hair out of her eyes for the millionth time. "I have my one piece suit on under my clothes."

"I have a bikini on," Anna said.

"Of course you do. Let's go down to the beach to the left of all those umbrellas."

They headed off in a smooth move over the long expanse of bone white sand to the water. Soon, they found a spot on the beach, far from the umbrellas, close to the water's edge. Rose swiftly disrobed and placed her clothes in her backpack. They had to keep their clothes dry and sand free. Rose tried not to stare. But most people were arrayed on deck chairs and blue and white striped towels that screamed *hotel*. Tan, well-oiled bodies gleamed in the sun. The men wore skimpy tight speedos. At least it wasn't Greece, where many swam nude. Rose forgot that she was young, beautiful, and free. She suddenly became so self-conscious about what she wasn't. Namely, European, elite, old, and wealthy. They were here though. They had made it. It was time to swim.

"Lets swim. I love swimming," Rose said. They sauntered towards the water. "Did I tell you of the time I swam naked under a full Moon in Greece? That was earlier this summer."

"You naked? I don't believe it."

"I was alone. And it was dark out."

"What? You swam naked, alone at night under a full moon?" Anna raised an eyebrow. "That sounds romantic."

"It could have been. I was in a small rock cove on Crete." She paused for effect. "It's just that the next day, everyone went on about sharks that inhabit the cove. Apparently the water is warmer there. That so freaked me out."

"If it's the right kind of shark it could be good," Anna smirked.

"Come again?"

"A wealthy one. Corporate takeovers and all that? To rescue you from the dark waters of a moonlit cove." Anna wiggled her eyebrows.

"I'm not a damsel. I can be romantic—alone. It's fun." She let sand run between her fingers like an hourglass. "Makes sense though, to have a boyfriend."

"You don't though, do you? Not at college, not back home. Strange isn't it?"

"I hadn't given it much thought. I like being single. Available. Not attached; especially while traveling, wandering around Europe. It's easier to meet the locals. I'm glad you are here with me Anna."

"But don't you see? Your letters home are full of such travels and adventure. You made it seem so awesome. And it is great. My home life seemed hard and boring."

"Now it's hard and exciting." The wind blew a cool breeze on her hot dry skin.

"Yeah, much better." The blue sea loomed before them. "Race you!"

Rose winked at Anna and they both ran for the surf.

Rose kept striding as she moved swiftly into that clean blue Mediterranean Sea until she was wet and in way over her head. Then she swam. The two sisters swam and swam. Anna swam the backstroke, the sidestroke and the crawl. Anna said, "Lets race."

The two raced parallel to shore. Anna was way ahead, but Rose kept a steady pace. She knew that they couldn't afford a room at any of the gleaming steel and glass hotels. She had a feeling that they might be *persona non grata*. In the meantime she swam for all it was worth. The sun glinted on the diamond peaks of the sea. The water clear and cool washed away all her fears and troubles for the time. Out of breath they both pulled out of the water and found a spot on the sand. All she hoped at this point was for the sun to dry her a bit before they had to go back.

"Now what Anna?" She wondered aloud. "I haven't thought this through. I don't see pensions' or Youth Hostels anywhere in sight."

"You're right. It's not America and I don't speak French."

"It's not the language here that's a problem."

"Listen, I hear Italian from that couple over there. The ones that gave us a ride were Swiss."

"The language here is money. We can't even pee here without cash for toilet paper. What about the 'Lily of the valley,' and 'God will provide,' and we are 'blessed creatures of God and Nature'?" Rose asked. She knew it sounded like a whine. Was she really all that spoiled by life?

"The French are snobs," Anna said. "You know that. Edith and Jean, and Stephan, they are family and they are all snobs."

They heard shouting and looked over where they had left their pile of stuff. Rose squinted in the sun and could barely see a guard–uniformed person yelling and pointing.

"Funs over."

The two raced over and smiled and laughed. "Scuzie scuzie. We don't speak French."

The guard with his tight lips was not amused. Anna grabbed her Nikon and took a few fast shots.

"Angry man," she laughed. In a smooth move, they grabbed their packs and sauntered over to resume their walk on the promenade. They found another bench. Rose dug out a big shirt to throw on over her damp suit. Anna had a slim beige tunic sweater she buttoned half way.

"Looks like this is the end of a beautiful thing. I'm sorry Anna." The cold air and brisk swim had cooled them both off. It was later in the afternoon now and the sun had lessened. "I've got to run to the bathroom. Can you wait here? I'll check the room prices when I am in there. That hotel over there looks quaint; older and smaller. Perhaps it's a better bet."

"Go ahead. I'm enjoying the scene." Anna was absorbed in her camera now. Zooming in on a few of the patrons gathered at an outdoor café.

When Rose came back, Anna was chatting with a forty-something gentleman with wavy black hair.

"This is Bernard," she said, turning to Rose.

Rose smiled thinking she was joking, but no.

Bernard spoke English quite well. His accent was charming. "Where are you two staying?"

"We're not," Rose said in a flat tone.

Anna stepped on her foot.

Rose glared at her and smiled at him. "I was just checking in at that hotel, she pointed. "But it's booked. They're all booked. This is the season I guess. I hadn't thought about that when we decided to travel here."

"Yes. All of France travels in August. Everyone has

three weeks off for vacation. The hotels save their reservations for French speaking clientele."

"I see," Rose said gravely.

"We've come all this way," Anna said.

"Ce las vie," Rose shrugged and tried to look nonchalant. Her anxiety showed. She knew it. "I thought it would be great to come here. I didn't realize…"

"How could you know?"

"Things are very different in America," Anna said. "Its freer. Fewer rules. More space." She spread her arms encompassing the crowds, the beaches, the towns, and the hills in one broad sweep.

"Anyway, we are on familiar territory there. We know the ropes."

"Be my guests for dinner," Bernard said abruptly. "I insist."

"No. Absolutely not. We couldn't trouble you."

"I insist."

"Please Rose? Oh Please. It would be fun to have a proper French dinner."

"Well, we will have to get cleaned up." Rose looked down at her oversized shirt a little twisted in her haste. "We are still a bit wet or something."

"My place isn't far away."

"Oh, you're not in a hotel?"

"Oh no. Come with me. You can get cleaned up, and then we will go to dinner. You can tell me all about Texas."

Rose glanced at Anna. She'd obviously been talkative while she'd been gone. Rose looked over in the direction. About a half-mile or so away, she could see a marina. There were tall masts and lots of boats over there. She hadn't even noticed them earlier, just a natural part of the scenery. As they got closer she could see the boats bobbing along the piers. And yachts, large and white, gleaming in the late afternoon sun. Of course, Yachts. Between the hotels and the yachts, this was a very exclusive beach.

"We can't do that!" Rose cried alarmed.

"Let me introduce myself properly, I am Bernard Funacello. I am happy to invite you two young ladies to refreshments at my place. It's not far, and after, to dinner and dancing in the Grande Hotel."

"Dancing?" Rose's eyes lit up. He had found her weak spot.

"I am a lonely man. I have been traveling for weeks and would love the company. No strings attached."

Rose glanced at Anna, looking for a sign. She was in her element, clearly charmed by this man. She obviously trusted him for some reason. She was a big reader of vibes. Or maybe it just felt good to stroll past the entire world as if they actually belonged here. Just ten minutes ago she thought they would be exiting stage left. But now?

8

RIVIERA

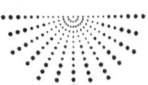

*T*he sisters became talkative as the mood turned festive. As they strolled along the shore, Rose almost bounced on the balls of her feet, as she took in everything, studying the harbor with piers, boat docks, and the array of colorful fishing boats: schooners, sail boats, and yachts. Rose felt like dancing. She breathed in deeply and her neck lightened as tension left. She felt cooled by the light breeze on the relaxed stroll with their new friend, Bernard. Seagulls flew low and accompanied the pungent odor of fish with a squawky tune. Bernard asked, and Anna told of their adventure.

"Where are we going?" Rose finally asked. She glanced at the three and four story townhomes that lined the promenade atop the outdoor cafés and small shops. All the buildings were colorful painted stucco with balconies overlooking the sea on this side of town.

"Just over there, around the bend." Bernard pointed past the fishing boats. "I am not a local, just stopping here for a couple of weeks. My friends insisted on meeting me this trip."

"Oh, do you travel a lot?" Anna asked.

"Just over there." Rose followed his finger. Past the swarm of gulls and spotted the slender white masts of moored sailing vessels.

"I hope you don't mind the stroll? I love the harbor this time of day."

"Of course not," Rose said. "I agree it's quite wonderful."

A fisherman struggled with his nets and pulled them aboard. A child ran after a small dog leaving his parents behind. Rose relaxed in the homey scene and opened up to Bernard, telling him about her studies.

"I was immersed in Art history class in Texas, squinting at slides in a class that everyone was snoring through, I thought, this is ridiculous. To look at pictures of cathedrals, the likes of which don't even exist in America, and poor reproductions of great paintings, is not brilliant. I thought my money would be better spent seeing it all in person. University is pricy you know? So time for a trip. Here I am. I've been traveling for over three months. All the art across Europe is now marked indelibly into my brain. Along with all the interesting people I met, meet—and local food to go with it. I have spent the whole summer in museums, from Edward Munch in Norway, to the British Museum. My sister Anna has rescued me out of the dark corridors of old castles and out into the sunlight of adventure." She stopped abruptly as she was out of breath.

Bernard smiled appreciatively.

"I was getting a bit lonely, I admit," Rose said. "I was so glad to see her when she found me."

"Lonely? You? You're so young. Surely you have made many friends or companions to travel with?"

Rose stared off at the sea remembering—all the faces passed like ships in the night. She, so focused on her planned agenda. Shrugging, she slanted her head up at him to see if he was kidding with her. "Anna has saved me. We are having fun."

"You two are unbelievable. I think I like Americans."

"Texans," the sisters chimed together.

"Texans. You should know, I have a few paintings on my boat."

Satisfied in their newfound camaraderie, the three linked arms.

If Rose's feet were sore she didn't know it. She felt that she was walking on air. "Aha," she teased, "you want to show me your etchings."

"Ah ha. We have arrived," Bernard said.

"What?" Anna exclaimed, "You are sleeping in that grass hut by the pier?"

"No. That's a bar. There." He was somewhat amused.

Rose looked up. Bernard pointed to one of the three yachts moored in a row, just beyond the shore.

Rose, struck speechless, opened her mouth and closed it. Anna and she carried their shoes as they walked barefoot along the sandy beach to the gangplank.

Anna smiled. "Looks nice."

Understatement, Rose thought.

"Welcome to my home away from home," he bowed.

The two tiptoed up on the pier and walked along the gangplank that led to the vessel.

Rose could hardly mask her surprise with such a wide smile. "Gosh are you sure? We are so sandy and uh—windblown." She'd been eating her hair between sentences. A sign she'd talked too much. He'd egged them both on, she knew. He was slumming it a bit by inviting them. They dusted each other off the best they could—before following him aboard the boat.

Rose put her sandals back on and adjusted her army

pack a bit self-consciously. The two trailed Bernard toward the sound of voices. A mixed group of men and women, cocktails in hand were gathered on the top deck. Although of mixed ages; all were over thirty and wearing success like a birthright.

"Welcome aboard '*Little Princessa*.' As promised, a place to relax before dinner." Bernard was eager to please them. "Okay, time for refreshments. What are we having?" He rubbed his hands and looked expectantly around while all his friends had gone completely and utterly silent. "We are just in time, I see."

"Water sounds good." Rose broke the silence.

Obliging immediately, Bernard told the waiter person-Rose assumed he was a waiter, "Three waters please. And what else? We have Bordeaux, Chablis, what is your pleasure?"

"I like red wine," they said in unison. Only Anna said "white" to Rose's "red."

"Great, Javier, meet my little refugees. Anna and Rose."

"We're not stow away's…yet."

Raised eyebrow.

"Kidding." She beamed a huge smile at him, begging forgiveness for any perceived affront.

"Let's see, we need a few Hors d'oeuvre's." Bernard took a double take at Rose's grin. "Anchovies, olives Nicosia… some salted almonds. How about a roasted beet salad?"

"That's perfect," Anna said.

"Please don't go to any trouble," Rose said, her mouth watering.

Bernard turned to Rose, "You look quite tan."

"She spent the early summer in Greece. Swam nude under a midnight moon," Anna offered.

"Aren't you poetic all of a sudden," Rose blushed.

Ever the gentleman, Bernard pulled out a deck chair for Anna at a round table and Rose seated herself. This appeared to be Bernard's Yacht, or at least he was tight with the owner, as he had the air of one who owned the place. Everyone saluted and darted about in hushed voices at his appearance. Soon there was water with lime wedges, glasses of wine and a chilled bottle in an ice bucket. Rose relaxed so deeply into the cushions as she leaned back and sipped her wine, she was afraid Bernard might have heard her sigh of pleasure.

The rude guests kept their distance, peering over there ice-cube-clinking glasses. Everyone seemed to be suitably marinated in pre-dinner equality. After a lot of jovial banter and the introductions made, various camps had been set up. One group, all European jet setters, was all in for dinner in town at the Carlton Hotel. Dancing afterward at the Terrace was unanimous.

"It's a three star establishment," Krissy explained, she seemed to be in charge, playing hostess to Bernard's host. The other group, they seemed mostly older, serious, and male, planned to stay on the boat and drink their dinners.

"If these are his friends, no wonder he's lonely," Anna said as an aside.

"That's mean," Rose said.

The girls realized it was time to rinse sand off and get presentable. Krissy proved to be the best.

Krissy looked them up and down, appraising. She had Anna turn a bit this way and that. "I have just the thing. I am Bernard's...a...friend. Follow me to my quarters below deck." Her smooth iron-straight platinum blonde hair swayed as she walked ahead.

Before they could resist, she was pulling out cocktail

dresses, and flowing shawls, and sequined skirts, some of which still had tags on.

"Bernie is the best," she said drawing best out in her accented English Rose couldn't place. "I love him. You two must look bootiful tonight." Krissy's blonde coloring and tanned lanky frame put her as Scandinavian or Swiss perhaps. She seemed to be fluent in both Italian and German. And English of course. Anna didn't even have to try.

Rose smiled, as she waved her arm to clear the abundance of Chanel #5 in the air. Krissy kept holding stuff up for Anna to test the fabric against her skin. And cluck-clucking like her new mother.

"This is perfect for you, Cherie, try this on."

Anna held the dress up, wondering, "Where?"

Krissy said, hands on hips, "We're all girls."

Anna turned and slipped the blue shift over her head. Rose buttoned it.

"Splendid!" Krissy said.

Then she took a long look at Rose.

"I don't think I have anything. quite…Well your shorter. Just not feeling it here. Oh, here's another Anna. You will look amazing when I'm finished with you, Cherie."

There was by now a pile of five or six outfits that would look absolutely fantastic. Krissie finally relented and handed Rose a delicate shawl. The fabric was light as down. Rose hung it around her neck, unsure. Anna wrapped it around Rose, and twisted and tucked just so.

"Thanks, I feel transformed." Rose did. She was praying fervently that this night would last. Fantasy was a great drug. The reality of traveling on, could wait until tomorrow. Rose wasn't to know at that moment, her prayers were heard and answered. A crack in the fabric of predictability and fate was to happen. A window of opportunity presented itself. Would she step through?

After making a whirlwind of a mess, the three emerged dressed and friends. They headed back, strolling the corridor, arms linked through. On the way they encountered an older woman. Miss Yvette appeared to reign from her throne on the cabin floor. Rose thought she saw a small tiara peeking out from the piles of silver grey braids that wound atop her head. Her lips were drawn on perfectly in pink. Her earrings were the largest emeralds Anna had ever seen.

Bernard appeared, drink in hand, as though on cats feet. He kissed Yvette's hand ceremoniously. Anna and Rose were presented formally and kissed her on both cheeks. Anna reacted immediately to her cool cheek. "May I get a shawl for you? You seem a bit chilled."

"Oh, yes dear. That would be lovely." Her eyes clouded a bit. Her head remained regal.

Anna found a paisley shawl and draped the merino wool fabric around Yvette's shoulders, tucking it close around her.

"Where are you off too?" Yvette asked. In a strong French accent reminiscent of their grandma's.

"Bernard is taking us all to dinner. Some place called carl or…"

"Ah yes dear, the Carlton." In the pause that followed, Rose could see the far off gaze of memory in her eyes again.

When Anna noticed the emeralds she broke the silence, "I love your earrings. Emeralds are my birthstone," Anna explained.

Yvette nodded permission, and she bent to look at them.

"My husband, Pierre, God rest his soul, gave them to

me, an anniversary present. We didn't have children." Her voice roughened, "Bernie's my nephew."

"Quite lovely. Are you comfy? What about your feet?" Anna removed Yvette's shoes; anyone could see her swollen feet had been squeezed into them. Anna massaged each foot briefly. Then pulled up an ottoman and placed them one by one just so. She patted the shawl in place. All this was done with the lightest touch and much respect. Her actions did not seem invasive.

Rose watched a bit spellbound. She had not realized Anna had such dexterity in handling people. Yvette's face softened, the lines falling away, melted by the caring touch. Anna wasn't going to fall for all of Krissie's favors, when this Madame was the one truly in charge, after all.

Yvette motioned for Anna to come near. Anna bent her head. "Dear, you should order the Salmon Oscar. It is superb. Chef Pierre prepares it to perfection. And the onion soup is a specialty."

"Shall we bring something back for you?"

She raised a dark penciled thin line of an eyebrow. "I am well fed here. You dine and enjoy." She waved a spotted frail hand.

Bernard watched from the doorjamb.

"We are off, Madame. Javier will get you anything you need. Paul and the others are still on the upper deck."

"Bah," she said. "I'll outlive the lot of them. And then what?" She waved him off.

"You will at that," Bernard said.

Rose and Anna smiled a bit shyly and left with Bernard. Krissie, already heels clicking way ahead, joined them with Mirabelle, Ben, and Gerard. Gerard looked harmless and interesting, so Rose thought she would get to know him. She wasn't sure at this point who were a couple, or if everyone was flying solo. Or if it even mattered in these nouveau groups of friends that have known one another for years.

"Do you like to dance at all miss?" Gerard inquired.

Rose turned, "Miss? c'mon, call me Rose. As a matter of fact I do."

"Good."

"Bernard promised us dancing after dinner. Dancing is a favorite weakness of mine."

"Have you ever been to Terrace?"

"No. I have never been here at all. We arrived today. This is our first evening in Nice."

"They have the best dance floor, and the best DJ on the Cote d'Azur. Bernard is a pro. We have a bit of a competition going on. Krissie can't really find the beat unfortunately. Despite her *wow* factor."

"Wow?"

"She is almost six feet tall. As a top model, she had the *Oscar de la Renta* line all to herself for years."

So it's not Chanel.

Porkay?

"The smell, her perfume. Never mind."

"Okay."

"O-Kay," How can you compete with that? Rose, all of 5'6 thought.

"Do you do any Karaoke?" Gerard asked.

"No." Rose sputtered, "Why do you ask?"

"I thought all Americans love karaoke."

Rose shook her head. "Is it that obvious? I thought if I kept my mouth shut my looks didn't scream American."

"Well your mouth is not shut," he appraised her a bit. "With those dark curls, you could be Italian or Francoise. I know you are a Texan—your sister keeps bragging about it…and the back pack."

"OOPs, I don't have a purse." She looked sheepish. "So do you?"

"*Moi?*"

"Karaoke."

"Ah, yes. I am quite good at Sinatra. I love Sinatra, *New York- New York*." He did a little shuffle.

Rose spotted Krissy linking arms with Anna and Bernard, inserting herself between them. She actually tried to tweak Anna's cheek when she said "Cherie." And tossed her perfect hair.

As the group walked off the boat and into the warm evening and through the boardwalk to the street, Rose wondered if she was jealous of Krissy or Anna? Her mind must be playing tricks on her. Gerard began a few bars of serenade.

Rose giggled. She hated that, it made her seem sixteen. She couldn't always control it.

Krissy squeezed into Bernard, "Let's grab a cab, our reservation is for 8:30."

Cabs screeched to a halt. Bernard grabbed one and then another stopped and the rest of the party packed in the second one and they were off.

Krissy said, "Let's give our young friends a tour of the town."

"Oh, yes," Anna laughed. "I have been dying to see a view from up there."

Squeezed in the back seat, legs touching in the back of the cab, Rose felt safe. She felt accepted and part of something. The warmth of belonging flooded her being.

They wound and wound up through narrow streets. They finally parked at the pull-off at the top. The overlook gave them a fantastic view of the Mediterranean Sea below.

Everyone piled out. Anna had her Nikon out, and

ready. Rose un-wedged herself from the back seat and followed the others to the edge. The pull-off, framed by a low stonewall, opened to the view of sea and sky. Below, the cove curved around the Mediterranean Sea like a crescent. Low hills framed the sides and a mix of trees and lights dotted the edge like intricate lace. One day at a time, Rose thought, as she joined the others on the edge.

Anna took photos. She shot the view, the sea. Everyone lined up, sitting on the stonewall. Anna shot the group. Rose grabbed the camera and she shot Anna in their midst. Anna's head tossed back in *the look*, her outfit, expensive and striking. She wore it like a pro. Rose shot Anna and Bernard; Krissie and her hanger-on friends; all the guys together; all the women together. Bernard shot the two sisters. And that was that. The final composition in the series.

Gerard began doing his Frank Sinatra with renewed gusto. He had a great mellow baritone. Rose closed her eyes as the warmth of his smooth crooners voice—Sinatra with a French accent— wrapped around her. She began to dance. Dance was in her and sometimes it just burst forth. As she danced, and a few grabbed hands, the sun sank and the moon came up. Rose felt free and weightless. Krissie bobbed her head as if trying to dance.

"Wait. Time for dinner!"

They all scrambled back into the taxis. After asking the driver to play some Sinatra, they rolled down the windows and all started singing. Rose closed her eyes and listened to Gerard's deep voice, the tone enveloping her. "If I can make it there, I'll make it anywhere it's up to you New York, New York!" Everyone joined in the off key medley.

9

RIVIERA - DINNER

*A*s they finished the grand meal, Rose, felt her stomach pushing out and up in all directions. Rose watched as Krissy struggled with her roles of controlling the whole group, flirting with any single man, and rushing back to Bernard to resume her place. Anna's no threat; she's only seventeen, Rose thought. Yet no one knew that. Rose smiled as the play in group dynamics unfolded before her eyes.

A round of grappa's seemed to be customary between the meal and desert. Rose had never tried the licorice like liquor, but was grateful, as it eased her digestion immediately. Enough so that while everyone was debating the various economic policies, both Anna and Rose accepted and enjoyed the proffered Chocolate Mouse. She justified the forbidden calories as she planned to soon be dancing her butt off.

After apple tarts, coffee, and more grappa, it was almost midnight before the group arrived at Le Terrace. No matter how tired she felt, she had promised Gerard a dance. He had been drooling all over Mirabelle at the other end of the table as the night waned. She vowed she'd *show them*, when she finally got on the dance floor.

The maître de at Le Terrace escorted Bernard and his group to a prime table near an inviting, glossy, parquet dance floor. Mirabelle pulled Bernard up to dance. Once there, he did one of his gallant bows before lifting her hand as if to kiss it. Then he pulled her into a fast swing as the band-music played. She responded in kind, her high spiked heels spinning dangerously on the wood floor. She stayed on the beat like a pro as her curly blonde hair flew around, reminding Rose of a pet poodle with a toy. Bernard could really show his moves. His hips moved sensuously to the beat in a smooth rhythm. His face remained passive as he pushed and pulled and twirled and spun Mirabelle under his arm and behind him and back. It was a sight to see, chauvinistic as it was. When Bernard resumed his place at the table, he'd barely broken a sweat. Mirabelle, panting, out of breath, left to refresh her makeup in the ladies room. When she returned she batted her long lashes up at Gerard, she really worked her petite size. He casually stumped his cigarillo out before succumbing to her blue-eyed charm. Rose inhaled the perfumed smoke wafting around the table.

Then a popular David Bowie song came on and the dance floor became packed hard with bodies pushing into the surrounding tables. Gerard appeared at Rose's side and invited her to dance just as she was wondering if sleep were on the menu tonight. He pulled her out onto the center of the room and the two were off. She felt like Ginger Rogers to his Fred Astaire as he twirled her. His straight longish blonde hair flew in bold contrast to her long dark unruly curls. The two spun around and around like a merry-go-round. Then Sinatra's voice crooned over the speakers and the two waltzed.

A space began to clear, forming room for Gerard and Rose to dance. Gerard steered her around, folding her in his arms, and cradling her from behind as they moved in unison. Then he pretzeled her around to face him and he spun her out and back in. On the outs she had enough space to extend her leg or add a few twirls before spinning back in on the next beat. Her dance skirt spiraled in and out around her as she spun around.

The night passed in a whirl of dancing and more dancing. She couldn't stop. Gerard finally needed a break and they both dropped back into their seats at the table.

Musky cologne entered her space, as Bernard leaned in to ask her to dance. "As I promised."

Rose hesitated a brief second. This was a slow dance. What the hell, she thought. She followed him out to the crowded dance floor. Then came the rhythmic sway as they moved as one to a Brazilian Bossa nova. A space as thin as a sheet of airmail paper remained between them. Imperceptible. Rose was acutely aware of his presence and the lightest tickle of stubble as it brushed against her cheek. She copied his stoic expression, as he led her around the room in smooth swirls and dips. She took all her cues from him. Like a mirror. Like his twin.

THE SECOND WIND KICKED IN WITH SUCH A VENGEANCE Rose was afraid if she stopped dancing she would simply fall over. Finally, Rose needed water and rejoined their table. She realized Anna and she had become quite a hit. All this went to her head and she didn't notice they'd made a few enemies in the process. She felt pleasure warm in her breast. She wasn't aware of Krissy's frown as she adjusted the shawl she'd casually tossed over her chair earlier. Instead, Rose shrugged to herself and now snuggled into the scented with French perfume shawl the glamorous Krissy had let her borrow. Krissy stared at her under long thick lashes. They're false, Rose suddenly noticed. Krissy blew smoke rings. Her eyes were perfectly made up with midnight blue shadow and dark moody eyeliner. Rose knew if she were wearing makeup, it would be running down her sweaty face by now. She excused herself to go and wash her face. Anna followed her to the bathroom; it was time to regroup.

Rose splashed her face at the sink. Anna came out of the stall and watched.

"Anna that outfit looks great on you." Rose smile was dreamy.

Anna shrugged.

"You having fun? Oh you're tired. Sorry I got carried away."

"I know you are." Anna scrubbed her hands with the perfumed soap.

"What do you mean? Dancing? It's so late now, what are we gonna do? Where are we gonna tell them to drop us when all the fun's over? We are turning back into Cinderella with her pumpkin coach and I'm afraid we missed our coach."

"So glad you asked. I was beginning to think you weren't worried about it." Anna rearranged her wide belt, studying her look in the mirror. "You know Bernard's been picking up the tab all night. He's covering for us."

"I am grateful. I'm having such a blast."

"Look, you know Bernard invited us back to the boat tonight." She leaned against the black and gold-papered wall. "There is no way I'm having another night sleeping on the road. He knows we don't have a place and he is being very generous. Most of the others are staying at the

Petite Mansion. It is a favorite local hotel. Exclusive. Those in the know, kill to get a room."

"How do you know?"

"He invited us. He knows we don't have a room." Anna waited a beat as she observed her sister dry her face. "I've been taking care of things sister. I have been getting to know everyone, while you have been," she rolled her big eyes, "prancing around on the dance floor."

"Thanks, I owe you." Rose smile was exuberant. "I didn't want the night to end, I was thinking if we stayed out late enough soon it would be morning." Her words tumbled out.

"What then? Sleep all day on the beach? You are unbelievable. You know that? Well not for me. Much better idea to take Bernard up on a good night's rest. Don't you agree?" Anna studied her sister's face.

"I am your big sister. We don't know him. If anything happens to us, I'm supposed to be the responsible one."

"Wouldn't I get a vibe? If we were way off base."

"You got me there sister. Hi – five."

"Hey sis, you look like you want to argue the point. But hey, let's just relax, smile, and let someone do something for you for a change."

"Relax?" Rose laughed, too tired to argue. "You're right, I'm not feeling very responsible."

"Look, I'm a kid. I am so excited about going back to that boat and sleeping in and having a great shower in that marble bathroom. Just let it happen and enjoy it."

"I am grateful. Supremely." Rose had put herself thru college so far. She was proud of herself for that. Making it despite the lack of funds had become the norm of her teen years—ever since the divorce. Anna could read her mind, and she had prepared herself well.

When they got back to the table, Krissie was sitting in

Bernard's lap. She bent over him to help herself to one of his cigarettes in a silver case, exposing her small breasts in his face while she struggled with the clasp. He expertly opened the silver case for her. She extracted one and waited for him to light it. She blew smoke in his face. He glanced away. When one of the Swiss brothers offered his hand, Krissie rose languidly from Bernard's lap, and followed him to the bar to shoot a row of tequila shots.

Spent from dancing, too tired to talk, Rose watched Bernard across the table as he removed his glasses from his jacket and studied the bill. His eyes clicked down the long tab like a mathematician. She noticed the slight crows feet at the corners of his eyes. He scrawled a number, totaled the sum and signed with a precise flourish. He was pretty sober she realized despite the *party* crowd he was with. She wondered if this was a special event or if there was always a nightly escapade into town. Krissie was still at the bar. The white linen tablecloth now a mess of empty tumblers and half-finished glasses, a jumble of lipstick smeared napkins and a few ashtrays with crumpled butts and ashes. A trail of cigarette smoke floated in the air. Bernard glanced up and caught her watching him.

"Thank you for a most memorable evening. I can't tell you how much fun this has been," Rose said.

"It is all my pleasure, my pleasure," he smiled as he replaced his wallet. "You my dear, are quite a dancer."

"I studied with Patsy Swayze in Texas. She's Patrick Swayze's Mom. But I do it all for fun now."

Bernard took a last sip of his cocktail and wiped his mouth. Rose noticed for the first time his ring, a small gold band on his third finger. Who was Krissie? she wondered. His girlfriend? Certainly not his wife. She'd let that go. Her head was spinning and it was none of her business.

"I've been meaning to ask you..." Rose began, then

Gerard appeared, offered his hand and pulled her back out to the dance floor.

"Another time," he smiled as she backed off out to the floor for one last dance of the night.

BY THREE AM, THE PARTY WAS BREAKING UP. TWO OF THE women they hadn't met disappeared with the Swiss brothers. Bernard gallantly held the chair for Anna. Rose downed two glasses of water back to back to quench her thirst as she rose from the table. The group piled out to the street. Gerard and Mirabelle told Bernard they were ready to walk back to their hotel. Ah Gerard and Mirabelle are an item after all, Rose noticed. Hard to tell that. The pang of disappointment hit her in the gut. I was really starting to let myself go on the dance floor. It is like we were so in sync he could read my mind.

"You two are coming with me. I have called the boat and your rooms are ready." Bernard once again assumed his position between them. "No argument from either of you. There is plenty of room."

He called out to Krissie, "We have lots of room right?"

Krissie was strolling with Danny and Tomas, friends that had joined them at the club. "Of course, dears. We are counting on it." Her perfect hair swung as she tossed a look at Bernard.

What does that look mean? Rose wondered.

Anna said, "I'm having the best night of my entire life. Honest. I've never slept on a boat before."

By the time they were back on board and tucked in, Anna was beginning to believe the Cinderella life was about to transform her.

"I was a bit worried," Rose said. "My usual luck is all about musical bedrooms."

"See? There is no problem, he has a girlfriend," Anna said.

"We can say our goodbyes gracefully tomorrow."

The sisters felt like two princesses as they each fell asleep before they could utter goodnight.

10

ROSE AND ARCHITECTURE

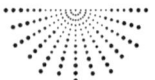

*T*he azure sky matched the Mediterranean Sea. Another perfect morning as the girls breakfasted on the top deck. No one was around yet. "I'm ravenous," Rose sipped her orange juice.

After a few days of being totally spoiled in the unaccustomed yacht living, Rose looked up at yet another cobalt sky. It was amazing how easy it was to adapt to this new awesome lazy lifestyle. Rose stared at the flat line on the perfectly flat water that divided the two. As she stared, she stated matter of factly."We are leaving today."

"No, Bernard and I made plans last night. He is taking me to Old Town." Anna stirred her eggs around a bit, "For a photo shoot. He thinks we should sort of write a story and then act it out in pictures. We'll give everyone parts— like a series of still shots. It's because Krissy loves to model. She is afraid she is on the way out as all the young bloods are stiff competition."

Rose looked up sharply, Krissy was being very accommodating to Bernard's attachment to them. She must feel threatened. Anna *is* the young blood. Krissy is hiding it well. "That is a creative idea. Who's?

"I told them you were very creative. Bernard wants to include you."

"I've only talked about writing. It's a hobby," Rose wailed.

"It's your opportunity."

"These guys have standards! I'm a novice. We are both...I'm not a performing monkey."

"I was thinking of you."

"You know, it's a great idea." Rose changed her tune. "You're right. I would love any old excuse to see Old Town. We came her to explore, see the sights."

"It's where the locals go. Not the tourists."

"Sounds like you guys are becoming friends." She smiled at her sister and ignored the fact that she sipped her juice and ate her eggs never touching any of the bacon, fried potatoes, and assortment of almond croissants that spilled out of the blue napkin in the basket.

ANNA HAD LITTLE TROUBLE CONVINCING ROSE TO SEE THE merit of the proposition. After all, she had no real reason to leave, just a vague sense of mooching and not earning their keep. They hadn't earned this lifestyle or even been born into it. On the other hand, Life was a journey—one she didn't want to miss. Rose smiled and relaxed, putting the big sister act away for a bit. "Tell me about Old Town."

"I haven't been there yet. But Bernard says there are some for real Roman ruins there and a giant Aqueduct."

Rose's creative mind flew into gear. "An Aqueduct? Wow we could choreograph a kind of dance number if we could have about six or eight people. It would be shot as a series of stills, of course. It would look just like a 1940's dance number." Rose forgot about Anna's strange eating habits as she considered the new opportunity. "What a contrast. You know, West Side Story style jazz moves on a Roman aqueduct. You could shoot it from in the bridge and from down below." Rose ran around as she spoke. "What do you think?"

Anna smiled and crossed her arms.

"We could raid the vintage stores for cool hats and scarves. And then perform on the bridge. How many guys could we get?"

"Gerard and the Swiss brothers love to dance, and show off. I think they will be into it," Anna said. "What do you have in mind exactly?"

"I would teach everyone some very basic stuff, Jazz walk, a few spins. It's all for fun right?" Rose was enthused. "We could throw in those ballroom spins and turns everyone is so good at. I will shoot too, so you can be in some of the shots. You can photograph all the guys, that way I can get everyone in position."

"I love doing candid's like that. I could get some good shots while they are learning the dance." Anna looked thoughtful. "Dad is the master of candid shots. I learned a lot from him."

"And some of it is instinctual. At any rate. If we can find a vintage place…"

"I'm sure there's one."

"Costumes help everyone to kind of get loose and get into character."

"These guys are already loose," Anna laughed.

'Roman Aqueduct, Pont du Gard,'

Anna told Krissy the plan and they grabbed a cab and headed out to the vintage store. The three ran in as if they owned the place—women on a mission. Anna found some wild colorful ties. Rose grabbed a polka-dot umbrella. All three went wild in the hat department.

They had men's felt top hats, fedoras, straw boaters. For the women there were sleek models with feathers and one had this netting with little sequins on it. There were large floppy brim hats and hats full of bows. Rose liked costumes; she liked the whole role-playing thing.

Once they were back outside, Rose said, "Wait gloves."

She had just run past a glass display case. They crowded back inside; she saw dainty white Sunday gloves. That reminds me of Marcel Marceau, Rose thought. The shopkeepers' mustache twitched. His grim demeanor didn't dampen anyone's enthusiasm.

Gloves; long ones up past the elbows, short leather ones, arm length satin ones, and fingerless ones. Bills fluttered to the counter as Krissie paid for the whole lot of stuff. The piles of accessories were piled into big shopping bags. Rose had even found some striped suspenders.

They headed out into the brilliant blue-sky day again to entice the others to join their latest escapade. Rosé knew with the costumes and the setting the event would feel like a story told in pictures. But what about a villain? She glanced over at Krissie. When Anna had told her the plan earlier she had embraced it. She was on board with purse in hand and had added insights of her own. "Krissie, who do you think out of this lot could play a villain?"

"Who is on board so far?"

"Well, we have Gerard, Mat and Dave, the Swiss brothers, three women. That way each gal has two escorts," Rose said.

"We need Bernard," Anna said.

"He won't do it." Krissy spoke in a flat tone that said hands off.

"He's got to. He's coming out with us," Anna said. "The location is his idea after all."

AFTER A GREAT DEAL OF FUSS AND ELABORATE COSTUME changes, Krissy put everyone in make-up including the guys. Finally, everyone was dressed and loaded. Then they were off, headed out to Old Town. Matt and Dave had their own car so they loaded all the extra supplies with them. Along with the costumes, they had baskets full of picnic supplies, cheeses, pate, fruit and several bottles of wine. Rose was working, so she stayed in her summer attire of pink shorts and oversized gauzy white shirt. A new wind off the sea started up, blowing everything and tugging the umbrella almost out of her grip. That would add a bit to the drama, she thought, as she watched the clouds in the sky race overhead. The villain character can wear the top hat. Very distinctive. She had the black dance skirt with her. Perhaps that could become a cape of sorts.

ONCE THE TWO CARLOADS ARRIVED IN THE TOWN, THEY orchestrated the best approach. Anna climbed the aqueduct and studied camera angles. Rose demonstrated some moves, choreographing on the spot to the music in her head. She then went through her moves with the group.

"Gerard has his boom box with his mixed tape with all his favorite Sinatra and Barry Manilow, even some Tom Jones songs loaded," Rose explained.

The sound kept being swallowed by the wind. The entire dance would be captured as a series of still shots, but dancing like they meant it made a big difference. Dancing in real spaces, was so inspiring to Rose. Architecture inspired, rather, informed the dance. As she worked, with the modern bodies in the ancient space new ideas began to flow. She danced with Gerard to demonstrate the moves she was creating on the spot. This is kind of like performance art, accept there was no performance, or audience for that matter. It was a pity it would never be performed. But it would serve her purposes. Or Anna's rather. They were becoming a creative team together. A series could look like a dance. All of it would take a week to rehearse if they were to do it for real. Rose choreographed several scenes where Krissy was completely surrounded by guys. Krissy wouldn't have to move much. She had her look and she had mastered it. Rose arranged them in a pyramid flanking her.

Bernard refused to dance, but he seemed to have great fun standing around on the sidelines. Rose took him unawares and did some Ginger Rogers dance moves with him. She handed him a rose, which he placed in his teeth. Then they did a few tango moves. Rose managed to startle him by fainting in his arms with a dramatic flourish, which had a sort of villainous flavor to it.

KRISSIE DID A JAZZ WALK STRAIGHT TOWARDS THE CAMERA. She was dressed to the nines with the long satin black gloves, a bright red scarf floating dramatically in the wind, and her hat cocked back just so. The two small figures in the background were an unsuspecting Bernard and Rose doing the tango as an unlikely Tom Jones crooned *what's new pussycat...* One part of the aqueduct held water, and Anna took a shot of the reflection that doubled the arch effect.

Finally, as the sun climbed to noon, when some were getting silly in the heat, Bernard announced it was time for the lunch break. Bernard opened the wine and Krissie pulled out the contents of their picnic. Rose lay back on the wall relaxing while everyone toasted each other. Anna took another shot of just the reflection, and a mirror image of Rose glinted wavy in the water. It was a peaceful image. Maybe Rose had a point. Anna was excited, convinced she had caught something good. There was a lot of great stuff on these latest rolls, having a creative eye was a challenge. Anna couldn't wait to see the prints developed. She would make sure to do it in town herself. She shouldn't send everything home to Dad. She chuckled at that. What would he think if she did? Perhaps she could send him a few of the extra prints. There would be plenty to choose from. She'd been well taught by her Dad. Shoot plenty of film to inure you have a good shot or two once you are back home.

11

FRICTION

"Where were you last night?" Rose's voice screeched in a way that hurt her own ears.

"Last night?" Anna asked.

"No last week," Rose said.

The girls felt like they almost belonged on a yacht after the success of the shoot. Anna planned to present some nice shots to Krissy once she found a darkroom. She was happy and content the night before. Everything had been quiet and Rose had done some watercolors of the sunset from her perch on the boat. Before she realized it was almost ten and everyone, including Anna, had gone on to do their own thing. Then she felt abandoned.

"Rome, Paris…" Anna rolled her eyes looking every-where but at her sister.

"Wrong answer." Rose frowned. "Anna, be serious, I was worried about you."

"We went out."

"Who? Who went out?"

"Bernard and Krissie. They had some people, friends

they invited…wanted me to meet." Anna hung her head. "I couldn't say no."

"You forgot to mention that small fact to your sister."

"You seemed happy! You love having time to work on your art. I know you need it. You were engrossed. Busy. I didn't want to disturb you."

"What time did you get back?

"It went a little long."

"I didn't hear you come in last night."

"I didn't want to bother you."

"You are no bother—my friend, my responsibility, yes. Are you going to tell me a nice story this morning about your adventure?"

"Sure. I'll tell all. Just don't be mad."

"Mad? Should I be?"

"Well they invited me. Not you."

Rose walked around in circles trying to get calm. She shouldn't take this out on her sister. "No, that's fine. I do spend hours on these drawings. It's awesome to have the time." She stared out to sea sightless. "When I went to find you. I couldn't. You had left and I was caught totally unaware."

"You've had your fun."

"You've had yours."

"Touché."

Rose stared out again at the flat sea. The water looked steely today, under a heavy grey sky. Nothing inspired her to draw today. All of a sudden she felt listless. She didn't have the energy to fake smiles. But she shouldn't let anger rule her relationship with her sister. She stared out far at the distant sea. Unsettled and unsure but did not know why she should be.

ॐ

SUNNY DAYS SOON MOVED HER SOMBER THOUGHTS AS THEY stayed as guests moored at the Riviera. Rose felt magnetized, she enjoyed her few encounters with Bernard. Mostly observing him from a distance. He took care of his business in his office each morning. Anna and Rose took off early to explore the various towns and sights. About ten AM they would have a nice swim in the glorious Mediterranean Sea. Anna usually went to hang with Krissie and her bunch in the afternoons which gave Rose the time she coveted at the shore. She'd found wonderful hidden coves and places near the harbor for her watercolor sketches.

12

PHOTO SHOOT

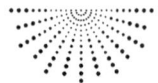

"*T*ime to head back to our real life." Rose greeted Anna with what was uppermost on her mind.

"Not me. This is a gold mine for me here. You can see that. Krissy and Bernard can make all my dreams happen —here, now. I don't even need modeling school." She joined her sister at the bow and they both looked out to Sea. "That's your problem you know. Too much school."

"I'm in University—taking a break from university. That is different than Modeling school, for chrissake." She pronounced modeling school with a British accent.

"If you keep on, soon you will be teaching—a perpetual drop-out of real life. Waiting for life to happen. Instead of taking it on; doing it. These guys are *it*. My dreams can come true!"

Rose paused, Anna could be right, this could be her break, but she had to convince her otherwise. "This is not real. This is an illusion—all the attention, false promises. It's a game for them. We will leave while we are still fresh. A guest is like fish— starts to smell if it's around too long."

"No. I have the look. I have *It*. It's my European features mixed with my American style. Texas. They love Texas out here."

"Why do you want to be a model anyway? Models are done at 25 dead at 30. Look at Krissie."

"Don't talk about my friends."

"They are beyond rich. They lose more money than we spend in a year. It's a different breed. Nothing is free. People aren't generous." Her tone was scoffing, as if she were somehow better.

"I can pay anyone who helps me, back. Do you have any idea how much a top model makes? A runway model?"

"Wait. What exactly did they tell you? What are they promising?"

"Krissie is going to introduce me to her agency." Anna looked smug.

"Which agency?"

"I can't remember."

"Ha." Rose crossed her arms. "Details, Anna, details. What do we really know about these guys?"

"You've changed your tune."

Rose ignored that, "What if the agency says no? That is not a guarantee. Nothing is free. There is a price. Mark my words." She was incensed. "And I don't want, I don't want..."

"Your jealous."

"No." Rose tone softened, "I just don't want that price to be you. God, Anna your backbones protruding. Aren't you eating at all anymore?"

"I want to look good for the agency when Krissy takes me."

"What about, 'you're only as young as your spine is

supple?' It takes food to be healthy. It takes health to be beautiful." Rose felt like Anna no longer heard her. "Who are you kidding? We are dolls. Play things. Why do you want to be a model? You didn't answer that. I was just humoring you before. It's not creative. It's boring. Passive. Models walk around in drug induced stupors-with vacant empty eyes. You are a talented photographer. That *is* something. Models have a flash of success then it's over, they're done, caput. All the make-up caked on can't change that. Look at Krissy."

"So do, do look at Krissy." Krissy sashayed in without miss step. "How do you like my new dress?"

Rose froze. She turned to see Krissy.

"Anna, Cherie, you promised I could take you out shopping. Alain promised he would be joining our party tomorrow evening. Krissy will make you fantastic. If Alain likes you, you're in." She turned and stared at Rose, one long frozen look.

"Run along now Rose. Don't you have some work to do, or museum to visit? We don't want to bore you with girl talk." She turned all her attention to Anna. Rose knew she was dismissed. Krissy tilted her head at Anna, "Something soft. No angled—tailored- Channel-ish. That would be right for your first meeting. I know just the shop to start with. You come with me. We will spend the entire day. We will have lunch at La Maison ." She circled Anna like a shark, with long strides and an intense gaze. She picked up her hair, put it down. Clucked and rubbed her hands together.

Had she heard them? Rose wondered. She stood speechless; Anna was clearly smitten by all this attention. Rose felt helpless. She couldn't explain anything to her little sister. Rose had some idea about how the world worked. She'd seen it with Aunt Jane back in California. Aunt Jane offered to send Rose to art school when she was nineteen. She had just begun Architecture school and she was a double major. Complete tuition to California Arts plus a place to live in California. Jane's beautiful mansion had been used as a movie set for some films. Aunt Jane had tons of money. Rose could have accepted it, and Rose would be on her way to an art degree from a prestigious University by now. That summer she had spent with Aunt Jane had been fine. But she had been sucked dry somehow. She couldn't name it, or place it. It was some kind of soul sucking feeling. Like her lifeblood was seeping from her. She was held like a prisoner of luxury and boredom. The good news was she had tons of drawings to show for her time there. And then when she'd escaped—somehow got away, she just couldn't go back. It was like Aunt Jane's money had all sorts of strings attached to it. She had sensed it; the way Jane stared at her when she swam laps and sunbathed beside the huge pool. It wasn't anything tangible she could describe. Perhaps her life would be completely different now had she'd gone down that path. Aunt Jane wasn't her real Aunt, she was her Uncle Toms 14th *wife*.

Her Uncle was the gigolo. Not her. Her Uncle, that was another story. He was so gorgeous, talented, and in supreme physical health. All of his carefully groomed looks to cover up his supremely insecure, Machiavellian personality. He'd gone to Hollywood in the 50's to *be* somebody. Rose had been his favorite niece, so he'd shared a few secrets when she traveled out to Santa Monica to visit her grandmother and him. What do you call the niece of a professional gigolo anyway?

Krissie glanced over with that look again. She waggled

her fingers at her "Run along now. We don't want to bore you."

Sugar sweet she could be. Rose walked slowly over to the door. She glanced over at Anna for a nod, something. Anna was completely self-absorbed, grinning and looking in the mirror.

TODAY SHE FELT RESTLESS, AND WANDERED IN AND OUT OF a few shops that she'd usually walk past without a glance. She drifted into a white washed lavender shop, with bunches of lavender spilling out of straw baskets. Lavender soaps and creams, lavender tea, along with drying bunches of lavender hung from wood beams in the ceiling. Rose walked out, heady with the scent and smacked straight into Bernard. Since their slow dance, he had evolved in her mind as some sort of mysterious and intriguing benefactor.

"You escaped your office," she said in greeting. Bright morning light glinted off the white stucco of the walls and warmed her smiling face.

"Fancy meeting you, again," Bernard said in his charming euro-accent.

They strolled side by side. Rose enjoyed the sunshine and this impromptu encounter. "Feels like déjà-vu, sort of," Rose said, as she slowed her pace strolling along the boardwalk.

Bernard engaged her with some charming small talk as he strolled, hands in pockets, his feet bare in butter leather loafers. To Rose it felt like slow motion. She paused in front of a dress shop she'd always wanted to check out, wondering how to say goodbye and move on.

Bernard said, "You never finished telling me how you enjoyed Italy."

She stared a minute too long at the intense blue eyes as

he turned his head to gaze directly at her. "Oh, Rome. I walked all over the city, which is a good way to get to know a place. I never did get to see inside the Sistine Chapel, I regret to say. It was off limits as the cardinals were shut in for Conclave to pick the Pope. Michelangelo's my favorite artist. He is both: an architect, painter, and sculptor. I saw as many of his works as I could."

"The David." Again he spoke slowly, in his charming accent.

They had stopped in front of a dress shop. She realized she shouldn't rush her speech as he wasn't a native speaker. Thank god he spoke English. "Of course I want to. I haven't yet been to Florence." The pink dress still hung in the window of the shop. It was pale pink with small roses all over it.

"Let's go in." Bernard pushed the door open. "After you."

The smell of lavender hung, smoothing out the noise of the street as they entered the hushed shop.

"I want to get you something. May I see that dress?" he said to the shopkeeper, pointing at the one in the window. The shopkeeper came back with two in different sizes.

Rose extended her arms towards the dress. The rich fabric was like nothing she'd ever had, silky to the touch. Her wardrobe was black, white, and blue jeans. She gasped at the thought of someone buying her clothes. No one had done that since she had turned fourteen and could work. The gift she shouldn't accept. But the dress was just perfect, she reasoned. Like it had been made for her.

"I can't accept this, but I will try it on," she said eagerly.

In the dressing room, once attired, it fit like a glove. She twirled around in front of the mirror; she enjoyed the feel of the silk against her legs. It made her feel feminine and pretty all at once. The color suited her skin tones perfectly. She came back out to show Bernard, she twirled around.

"It's a dance dress," she said.

"We'll take it," he nodded to the shopkeeper.

Eager to make a sale, she had it rung up, and whisked from Rose's fingers before she was back in her well-worn jeans and white gauze top. The shopkeeper wrapped it in tissue and placed it in a violet bag tied with twine and a sprig of lavender. Rose was flooded with emotion. Of course she'd accept a dress patterned with roses that fitted exactly. It made her feel more like a glamorous movie star than a dancer.

"Well you caught me." She patted her jeans. "I had intended to go out to sit on the rocks and sketch boats from the shore. Somehow, I felt too restless to sit still."

"Instead of the shore from the boat," he quipped.

"Have you ever tried painting waves?"

He stared at her as if to say something but decided not to.

"It's amazing," she gestured. "Like a city floating on the water. Anna's met her match and joined Mirabelle and Krissy shopping for the day." They resumed their walk. "I begged out to draw. And here you caught me."

"I too am playing hooky. I got a big windfall of good news. So I decided to get out and enjoy the sunshine."

"I'm surprised you can't do that on the boat."

"Believe me, when we are sailing, there is no getting off the boat. I like to feel my feet on dry land when I am moored."

"Ah, you're right." She squinted in the bright day. "Are you always right?"

He smiled and she took that as assent. He then steered her through narrow shady side streets.

"Here we are." Bernard stopped abruptly.

An ancient arched wood door thick with cracks and age was embedded into the stucco wall. He pushed gently and it swung open, revealing a small courtyard. The place was full of green spring grass around a stone fountain center. Hot pink bougainvillea hung in flowing planters and petunias scented the air. Lilacs and lemon trees grew in large earthenware pots. Wisteria hung in cascades from a trellised patio just beyond the courtyard. There were a few patrons dining seated at metal tables and chairs.

"Time for lunch," Bernard announced. They had missed the crowd at this hour.

"What kind of windfall?"

"Lets just say my ships come in."

"Ha, funny." The waiter gestured for them to seat themselves. Bernard pulled out her chair and Rose sat down. "What do you do for a living anyway? I mean don't tell. Excuse me if I'm being too personal. I just assumed..."

The waiter handed them each a menu and brought out carafes of water, small glasses and silverware. Bernard pulled out his glasses and studied the menu.

"Tell me." He looked amused.

"That you were one of those independently wealthy Europeans. Aristocracy and all of that, born to the manner stuff."

"That yachts just fall from the sky?"

Rose was really embarrassed now. She scooted around in her blue jeans wishing to god she was in the dress. "Gosh, I'm so stereotypical. I make too many generalizations."

"You are a socialist."

"Well yes, kind of. Like the rich will only get richer and its difficult for the poor to climb out of poverty. Therefore, if you have money now, it means you have always had it. Your family had it. The aristocracy, you know. Don't let anyone in. Don't share the wealth." She turned beet red. "I mean, obviously I was wrong about you."

"I let you in."

"Did you suspect?"

"You are a student and an idealist. You are young."

"My highest goal is to design a utopia."

"Ha, I knew it, you are a utopian idealist believing in a socialism that can never exist."

She let that go. "So you are different. You are a real person not a type. Just like I want to be seen for myself, not a gypsy. I don't want to be guilty of typecasting others. I see you work every morning. The others seem to sleep in and party way into the night. I see this. That's why I asked. I'm not sure of the protocol."

"I understand you, Rose. I am glad you let me buy you that dress."

Rose blushed again, "Thanks."

"Your welcome." The waiter brought the soup du jour. Bernard ordered the prix fixe meal. "The Chefs inspiration is usually the freshest things from market that day."

"And Wednesday is Market day," Rose said.

"You are catching on. Fresh is treasured when you are living on a boat."

Rose took a few bites of the clam chowder. "It had a hint of pepper in it that warmed her insides. Rose blushed. It was Queen Yvette and the tiara and the emeralds, putting it all together had given her the wrong picture. Tycoon begets tycoon. She would aspire to be one herself one day, that is if she were male, and/or interested in wealth. She was interested in Art and creativity—making things. All that took was time. She needed time. And time cost money.

"I'd love to tell you about myself, if you're asking." Bernard settled into his chair, in this delicious smelling courtyard. "I'm from a small town in Italy. I was very poor growing up, but no more so than anyone else in my village. There was no shame in it. It's just that I wanted more. I wanted to see the world. It was a fishing village. The boats would come from afar to our port. I would try to sneak on board to check things out and listen to the stories of the sailors when they lunched at the local cabana. Finally when I was old enough I was taken on by an old ship captain. I determined to work hard, save my money and buy my own vessel. Then once I bought my first boat, well it snowballed from there."

Rose smiled so big. She was full of admiration for this man before her. He was a self-made man. She loved self-made men as much as she despised the 'sons of wealthy men.' They seemed to walk around the world, full of entitlement.

As he told his story she could see that little boy he'd been so long ago, with that eager hungry look in his serious blue eyes. It's like he'd taken life on. They had that in common. He'd played the game—all in.

"Wa-la, here we are, together in the summer of 77, on the Riviera. It's a game of chance that our lives would cross at all."

Rose face froze mid-bite of today's catch; a fish poached in lemon, butter, and onion, so delicate in flavor. How had they met? It was Anna. Anna had found him in the brief five minutes she'd been gone. Her thoughts raced, she'd left Anna alone, a young 17 year old. He'd approached her. They had been well in conversation by the time she'd returned. Wait. She was getting loopy on the white wine and the sunshine. She would have to think on her feet. She smiled and commented on the food and the weather, to break the intimacy. He reached over and poured more white wine into her glass, the wisteria wafted a sweet scent in the air in a light puff of wind.

"Cheers," he said, encouraging her to lift her glass, although she was already feeling the buzz.

BERNARD AND ROSE

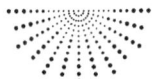

"Cheers."

She looked up into his blue eyes, which were suddenly too close. Again she saw the boy eager for approval, steely determination to, not just succeed, but to win, in the man. What character he had, she thought. She smiled a big generous happy smile. The wine warmed her to her toes as it went down. She glanced down, all the while feeling his eyes still on her. Studying her. I really want to wear that dress she thought. The fantasy in her mind had her dressed and dancing in Bernard's arms.

She laughed. "What are you thinking?"

"I'd like to take you out dancing in that new dress." His eyes never left hers.

"You can't take me out, we're friends."

"You think I'm too old for you. I'm not."

"Yes–of course, well you know," She was getting older by the minute. She'd aged three years in the last five months she was sure. "Well," I'm tongue tied she thought, "You're with Krissy. I figured that out at least."

"She'd like to think so," Bernard said.

"And you're married."

He smiled and sipped his wine.

"The ring."

"You are very observant."

"Most single women notice rings, but yes, I am observant."

"Krissy thinks I am. It works as a sort of protection for me. She's happy to play mistress to a married man. Keeps us both uncommitted."

"Wait, Krissy's your friend, she thinks you're married, but what?"

"Look, I am talking to you, telling you things no one knows. Yvette is a real countess, but she's not my real Aunt. It's complicated. Aristocracy- titles- money hangers on, wannabes. God it's complicated. Refreshing to get it all out."

The waiter appeared with cups of black coffee, and pitchers of steamed milk.

Rose glanced down at the raspberries and mint placed on the toasted top of the crème brûlée. She tapped the surface to break the crisp shell as she inserted her silver spoon. She placed the cool warm creamy stuff in her mouth, and again found him watching her.

"Oh, I thought you were married."

"I was. We divorced. I'm not proud of it."

"Oh, I see. How?"

"My parents are… It's not a pretty picture."

Rose looked around at the setting. The courtyard with wisteria dripping from the trellis and white blossomed jasmine clinging to the stone wall. She clung to this moment. She wanted this to be real. She felt it as her heart skipped a beat. She had wandered into his world, but it had nothing to do with her.

"This is a pretty picture." She breathed in the sight and

inhaled the scent of wisteria. "I'm glad you brought me here today."

"Yes. You are a pretty picture."

Rose twined her spoon around in her coffee, all but batting her eyes as she had seen the other women do. The only thing wrong with this picture, besides all the twisted tales, was he wasn't French and she so wanted to meet a French guy. Of course, all the other details. Fish boy to Playboy? There must be more to his story. She realized there were only a few stragglers left on the terrace. Bernard rose and helped her from the table. She picked up her pack and package.

"Shall we?" he asked offering his arm as they turned and headed in the direction of the boat.

She was honest for the most part and not into games, but she had her guard up big-time. She didn't want to let that show. Not while they were on his boat. She'd think of a way to convince Anna it was time. They'd had their fun. Bernard was a lot older than she. The same age as some of her Dad's friends, so she felt comfortable around him. But talking to a seventeen year old, standing alone. Why hadn't she ever snapped to that before? She knew why, even as she pondered. She wasn't as independent as she'd like to project. It was wonderful to be rescued by a handsome stranger.

ROSE WAS GLAD SHE HAD THE BEDROOM TO HERSELF *AFTER the long afternoon lunch.* The boat was quiet this hot summer afternoon. She sat on her bed and removed the carefully wrapped dress from the lavender tissue. She placed the fragrant sprig on her nightstand. She held the dress up and danced around the room.

14

EVENING ON THE YACHT

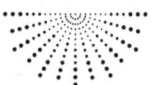

*R*ose made it back to the boat on an exceptionally hot afternoon. Her thoughts had been consumed with Bernard all day. She'd swam even harder and longer as if she could swim away from them. She usually liked leaving all that sea water in her hair. Today she was thankful for a place she belonged, at least at present, so she could shower and change. She was looking forward to relaxing on the upper deck with a front row view of the sunset. She had a feeling it would be magical today, and she was just in time. Now, cleaned and refreshed in a white cotton dress, grateful the boat was all but abandoned, she shuffled off her sandals, and tiptoed barefoot to her favorite spot. Surmising there was some event everyone was off to, and no one bothered to tell her about.

BERNARD WATCHED THE YOUNG GIRL/WOMAN FACING THE sunset, face in profile, lips parted in a half smile. She seemed so young and ageless at the same time. She faced the horizon with sunlight etching her features like gold filigree. She sat poised and still, becoming as much a part of the scene as the sun setting on a seashell. It had become so normal to have her here on his boat. Bernard approached with two glasses of chilled white wine, reluctant to interrupt. He felt a pang as he offered the glass of amber liquid and she turned with a look and a gasp of shock.

"Oh, I thought I was alone, you startled me." She glanced down at his butter soft Italian loafers. He was quiet as a cat.

"May I join you? It seems that the crowds have abandoned us yet again."

"Whatever shall we do left to our own devises?" Rose said, almost flirting.

"You can be yourself with me. I like you just the way you are."

Rose glanced down at her bare feet, she'd been balancing on the prow of the boat, knees to chest, toes pointed, face to the sea, like some sort of mascot.

"Oh Bernard, I wish I could sail away with you to that far horizon."

"I wish you could too."

He extended a hand to escort her down, and Rose put one hand in his, the other held the wine. She noted the golden sun caught in the glass. And she gracefully followed him to the rail. They both watched the magnificent sunset together, without speaking. Rose slowly realized she could be herself with this man. She didn't have to speak. Her mind raced to think of clever things to say. Words tried to burst from her ever-talkative mouth. But instead she stared at the magnificent presence of the sun as she sipped her wine, feeling the taste of sun in on her lips. She felt she could feel herself maturing on the spot, as the sun beckoned her to rise to the occasion. She felt herself grow taller.

Javier, the manservant, appeared with a tray holding the ice bucket and chilled wine along with the customary canapés of olives, anchovies, dates and salted almonds. Discretion. These accouterments were suddenly on a table beside two deck chairs.

Rose toasted. "When will you be sailing away?"

"Within the week. I am expecting a visitor, depending on our negotiations, I will most likely head for Spain."

"Where in Spain?" Rose asked casually.

"I have a small place on the island of Majorca. I will attend to things there for a week or two. It will be a rest after here."

"You do work a lot."

"Then I am back to Italy."

"The Mediterranean Sea is so beautiful."

"You have yet to see the Aegean Sea. There is much I could show you. There are so many wonderful hidden places one can reach by boat."

"Is it so beautiful?"

"It is my home." His fingers traced her slender wrist with a whispered touch.

"Hey, if the troops are ashore for the evening, shall we get Miss, Aunt, Yvette and bring her out here?"

"Splendid idea. You're observant. She avoids my friends."

"You avoid your friends."

"Touché." Bernard addressed his manservant. "Javier, please find Yvette and bade her join us. We shall have supper on the deck?" He glanced at Rose for assent.

"Oh, yes." Rose clapped her hands, "That would be delightful."

Javier saluted, "As you wish sir."

The stern woman was miffed. Her look was severe, as though affronted to be summoned at the whim of her

nephew. Her thin lined eyebrows raised the merest frac-
tion, and her lips remained a line, as she was jostled up the
stairs and out to the cool twilight air.

"Ah, it's you, and you, Rose." Miss Yvette's face softened and relaxed into the private comfort of just a three-
some. She breathed in the night and the evening.

As the evening ensued, Rose felt like she was part of
the family. She felt completely at ease. She was glad most
of the pretense was dropped. It was such an effort. The
three talked and listened to Yvette's stories of her upbring-
ing. As a single lonely child in an elaborate estate, her
friends had been birds, roses, and nature. All her love was
bestowed upon her widowed father who traveled much. He
loved her truly and doted on her, spoiling her when he was
home. Bernard had worked for the father and son team
when he was but a boy himself. He became almost an
adopted grandson. Bernard worked for him and climbed
up the ranks. When he became captain, he was able to
inherit the ship from the son. Yvette, strong willed, had
refused to be married off to various opportunistic suitors.

She'd even seen thru the Greek tycoon, Onassis, when
he came calling. "He'll find someone young and naive soon
enough," she'd said. "I could see straight thru his eager
opportunistic black heart," she told Rose who was hanging
on ever word, spellbound. "I already have what he longs
for but may never find."

Rose knew she was referring to the familial love and
loyalty that bound her family. The kind that miles and
months at sea couldn't weaken. Her father and brother
loved her enough to respect her wishes, and solitary simple
desires. She'd outlived them both, and Bernard, although
younger by 25 years, was now her companion. Rose was
fascinated by the stories of jet-setting in Monaco and
gardens on the islands of Sardinia and Majorca. Once

Yvette was a certain age, and fully established as a spinster, she had done a great deal of traveling. There is much freedom in being a singleton.

Rose pondered her words. She herself had been on a great adventure this summer just traveling alone prior to meeting up with Anna.

15

MIDNIGHT PARADISE

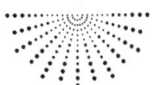

*R*ose opened her wardrobe and found herself staring at the new dress Bernard had given her. She held it up, wondering if she would ever have a place to wear it. When she heard a soft knock, she spun around and faced the door.

"May I come in?" Bernard's quiet voice asked.

"Just a minute." She lay the dress on the bed and went to the door.

"It seems we have been left alone this evening. The boats eerily quiet up there. Is Anna gone too?"

"She had a meeting with Krissy. Don't know how long it will take though."

"Krissy's a pro. She's probably getting her a complete makeover and a day at the spa. Being beautiful is a business expense in her profession."

"Care to join a lonely old man top-deck?"

"Of course." She blushed crimson again. Between blushing and giggling she seemed young for her 21 years. "Not that you're old, or lonely…"

"After you put that dress on."

"Aye, aye captain," she saluted.

"I'll be upstairs."

Rose rushed; she didn't want to miss happy hour. The sunsets here were spectacular. When she appeared on the upper deck, true to his word, the place was quiet, only the lap-lapping of the waves against the hull. Rose watched Bernard pace, his gaze intent and out to sea. A silver ice bucket with a bottle of white wine chilled on a side table. He turned at the sound and gazed at her as she walked to join him at the bow. He was frozen. Just staring.

Rose glanced down a bit self-consciously. She then smiled and laughed and twirled to display the dress and bridge the awkward distance more quickly. The skirt spun around her, in pure perfection. He poured two glasses of the white wine and offered her one. They clinked glasses. She glanced around. "Where is everyone? I thought cocktail hour was mandatory."

"Perhaps there is a party and no one told us?" He sipped his wine. "I think we should hold tradition and enjoy cocktails on the boat. Later on I know a little place in Old Town. It's small, and perfect."

"Good," Rose said. "Perhaps Krissy and Anna will be back and can join us."

"Sure." He smiled and showed his dimples. She'd never spotted them before.

The wine tasted zingy on her tongue. She and Bernard hadn't spoken since the afternoon with the impromptu lunch. She hadn't even had a chance to tell Anna about the new dress. After another glass of wine and she'd devoured a plate of anchovies with olives and almonds, Rose was quite comfortable again. She told a few jokes that she thought were so funny she didn't realize that she was the only one laughing. She secretly hoped no one would show up at this point.

"Are you ready my dear?" Bernard offered his arm. "It's time for dinner."

Rose finished the last sip of wine. "Sounds wonderful, *une momento*," She put up a finger and excused herself for the ladies room.

Bernard nodded discretely to Javier who appeared to clear the table. While in the bathroom, Rose splashed her face with ice cold water and patted herself dry. She sprayed a bit of scent on and pinched her cheeks. When she joined Bernard back outside her heart skipped a bit. This felt like a real date. The two strolled from the boat out to the street. Bernard hailed a taxi.

The evening was young. They drove along the coast rode before ascending, winding up to the top of the hill to OLD TOWN. Rose glanced at Bernard. He probably hated being driven. She imagined him in a Ferrari or a cool sports car back home in Italy. His hands looked listless in his lap as though itching for the wheel. She studied his profile, the roman sculpted jawline with a hint of scruff. His face closed, unreadable. Rose thought about her first taxi ride with the whole group; she egging Gerard on. She was so subdued tonight by contrast.

The restaurant was part of a small hotel that was a converted castle. It jutted out over the bluff. The outdoor terrace had an amazing view. While Bernard ordered for them both, she studied the sky. He selected a bottle of red zinfandel without checking the list. He knew this place well, she surmised. The midnight-dark mountain shapes of clouds moved en mass across the twilight blue sky. The sun set leaving a rich blue, dark enough to watch each star appear like exclamations on a great day. She held her arms to warm herself. A light breeze wafted in as a big moon rose coyly, as if she was playing hide and seek behind the clouds. The oyster Rockefeller appeared with a whiff of garlic and parmesan. She smiled at Bernard. He lifted his glass. She glanced at hers. Deep burgundy wine was untouched. She hadn't noticed when he'd poured it for her. This definitely felt like a date, just the two of them, out here with moon, wine, and romance. Bernard was in a quiet mood. Rose had to check herself from blurting out too much, or the wrong thing. She didn't want to make assumptions. But how should she steer this conversation? Don't talk of Anna, he might think of Krissy. Not her family, that was off base. His work? Art?

"Starry, starry night," she said.

"Van Gogh," he said.

"We are in his world. Aren't we? Here in Provence. He must have seen a starry night like this one."

Then the floodgates opened in her mind. Crazy van Gogh. Or '*The Scream*' by Munch. "I loved Norway. I want to go back to see the Fjords." Pictures, thoughts, her travels for the past three months had been solo. She needed someone to talk to, someone to share all of this with.

"By boat is best."

"Oh yes, surely you've sailed there."

"I have traveled by water for years."

"What's your favorite place?"

"Hard to say. One loves Venizia of course."

"You are Italian."

"I prefer the Aegean sea. And the Amalfi coast."

"Your filling me with travel lust, and I am probably in the best place I have ever been right this moment."

As the patterns of clouds and dance with the moon made paintings in the sky above the choppy Mediterranean Sea, Rose laughed and talked and dropped any previous doubts about this man.

"Is something wrong? You are so quiet." Rose asked.

Abruptly, "I was thinking about where to take you dancing."

"This is my new dance dress after all," Rose agreed.

"Did I tell you, you look amazing?"

"Thanks. I feel good. It's a perfect night for terrace dining in the sky."

The waiter brought chocolate mousse for desert with two spoons. Lifting a spoonful he headed towards her mouth. She took the proffered bite of the rich creamy stuff. His face was in shadow.

She blushed at the gesture it felt so personal. "Yum. Your serious tonight."

"Be back in a flash." Bernard abruptly left the table. When he returned, the David Bowie song, '*Let's Dance*' began playing; a sharp contrast to the earlier House music.

"Shall we?"

He could read her mind. She wanted to dance. She just hadn't wanted to leave the magic of paradise. She didn't want the crowds and she detested the noise. As he spun her around the stone terrace impromptu dance floor, *neither does he*, she thought.

"I don't know if you noticed, but I am keeping you all to myself this evening."

"Thank you, it's lovely."

WHILE THEY DANCED, SHE FELT FREE—FREE TO BE herself and not at all self-conscious. He didn't judge her for her gypsy soul that craved freedom and expression. He knew she was a dancer; as in the use of space, expression, movement—joyful exuberance. In this small-rarefied café, hidden away in an old village, the tourists were nada. Bernard knew his way around the Cote D' Azure—the private, untouched, hidden and exclusive.

She felt so free. He could really dance. The last time they'd danced he'd been reserved. He could spin and tango and even swing when it called for it. He had the moves. And she could feel him driving her with just a whisper, or a breath. The only ones watching the show tonight were the waiter and the busboy. Perhaps the cook was on a break too. Having shut the kitchen down already. While they were talking she'd barely noticed the other activities.

They were on the edge. She was spinning and twirling close to the edge. When they finally dropped to the table to regain their breath, Bernard poured them both a Perrier. As he bent towards her, she kissed him spontaneously on the cheek. He turned towards her, and she got half a mouth. It was impulsive. But he seemed so young and approachable. Something about the way he let go on the dance floor.

"Dancing here is a metaphor for life. I want to live like this," she said. She smiled. The music was a moody French song, theme from the new film '*Bilitis*'. The wind blew her hair about her face and cooled her sweaty brow.

"With me?" Bernard's serious words broke the quiet.

She froze. The words hung stark in the air.

"I meant," she backpedaled. "Dancing on the edge. In the wind, in the night air."

"I live like this. Sailing is like going with the wind. I love it too."

The wind had whipped the sky clean. Now the moon shone huge and round with a big red circle around it.

"Time to head back." He offered her more water.

"It's" probably late. Thank you for everything." She bent to loosen her straps and removed her shoes. The cool cobble stone street felt good on her bare feet. Her hand felt safe in his big strong grasp.

"Wait." Rose stared at the deserted road. All the houses shuttered tight for the night. "How do we get back down?"

"I asked the café to call a cab. We can walk a bit if you like. I am sure the cabbie will spot us when he gets here."

The thought of hitchhiking was far from her mind. It's amazing how quickly one can adapt to a cushy lifestyle. She dared to hope those days were behind her.

WHEN BERNARD AND ROSE STROLLED CASUALLY BACK ON to the yacht. The lights were dim and things were quiet. Krissy sat alone at the bar crouched over her drink. It looked like just the latest one in a long line of martinis.

"Oh there you are, Bernard honey." She turned, pushed off the bar and sauntered up to them slurring a little.

"Hey. Is Anna back yet?" Rose asked.

"In her room." Krissy sniffed.

" 'Night. I will join her." Rose kept her head down as she tiptoed out in bare feet.

Krissy slipped into an armchair. "How about a night cap?" she asked Bernard.

Rose scampered down the corridor to her room feeling guilty. She rapped on their cabin door. "Anna?"

"I'm here."

As Rose entered slowly, she saw Anna looking gorgeous. She was all done up with a new hairstyle similar to her earlier swing, but fresh and daring. Her eyes looked huge, with all the layers of eye shadow and mascara.

"When did you guys get back?" Rose asked.

"Not long ago. We were at a party at La Mansione, in that arty town. Krissie is pissed because Bernard was supposed to join us. He never showed."

"He must have forgotten."

"On purpose more like. Let me look at you." She twirled Rose around to get a better look. She whistled, "Nice dress."

"It's nothing. You look amazing. So put together. You look older. Sophisticated."

"Krissie's been great to me. Look." Anna showed her an array of packages and items arrayed on the dresser.

Rose saw perfume, make-up, a purse, belts and more laid with care on the bed.

Anna was saying, "Lancôme, Channel, Cole Hahn, Juicy Couture…"

"Wow. She's gone way out."

"She charges it all."

"Was it great? The party and all?" Rose was stung at the obvious insult. "Why didn't you tell me about it. I would have reminded him, had I known."

"It's funny. I don't understand at all. But it seems when I heard them talking, she wanted Bernard to come. It was an important introduction she was making. She didn't want anything to spoil it."

"Spoil it?"

"Her big plans. I don't know. I met an absolutely fabulous Greek guy named Peter. She introduced me to so many people I can't even keep it straight. Then we came back here. I couldn't wait to see you…show you."

"Did you mean I wasn't invited to the party on purpose?" Rose felt stung. "What's up with that? I feel bad. I'm your sister. Why do you just want to abandon me?"

"It's not me. Krissie calls the shots. I wanted to bring my bags back, pick you up, she said there wasn't time. She didn't want to be late. " Anna paced, and stopped in front of the mirror captivated by her look. "Its not on purpose or anything. I just thought Bernard would bring you, naturally."

"Oh, I see. So you think he knew all along, and didn't want to take me? Is he, are they embarrassed about me? What's so bad about me?"

"Well, you are different." She stared back at Rose over her shoulder.

"You, on the other hand, are all made up to perfection. Ah well. I'm glad I get to see you all done up. I certainly don't want to spoil your evening. So tell me about this Peter."

"OK. He's 29. Kind of old but so-oo successful. He's a photographer for Vogue and he wants to shoot me. He gets to call a lot of the shots you know, choose his subjects. The others are sent out as needed on assignment. He makes his own assignments."

"Wow, that is really awesome news. On two levels."

"Yeah? How so?"

"I bet he has a studio, and a dark room. Where is he from? Does he live around here?"

"A local? No way. This is the scene. He's here to make the scene."

"Well, give me some details then. What's he really like?"

"Longish sun-streaked hair like Gerard's. By the way Gerard likes you, he was asking where you were. Anyway, deep brown eyes. A nice accent." Anna shrugged nonchalantly. "Your type. No biggie to me. I like to listen to him talk."

"Now you sound like me."

"Dresses neat. Blue jeans, boots, a sports coat. I think he's like us. Pulled himself up. Works hard, willing to do what it takes. An artist. He looks at me like he's looking into or beyond me. I can see his wheels turning, It's odd. It's different. He likes my look. That's what counts." She shrugged.

"I get it. He sounds cool."

"I met so many people. Next time you have to come. Krissie was parading me around like a pet poodle at a show or something."

"Maybe she thinks she's inventing you. Has some sort of ownership."

"Like she got mad when I spent too much time with Peter. I don't know, jealous or something? Almost as if I was supposed to stay with her and nod and smile on demand. If I hadn't met Peter, I wouldn't have had any fun really." Anna was quiet as she thought about it. "It's like what you said about the object thing. In my mind I wanted it. To be this beauty that could make money just being me. Then when I got back here to the boat, I wanted you to see the total affect. So I couldn't relax. Look. I can barely sit down! It's funny really. I can't wash my face."

Rose jumped up. "I got it. Here, get your camera. There are some huge full-length mirrors in the stateroom. We could go in there, and you could take some self-portraits. I can take some too. You have a good eye. You can direct me. First, I need to wash my face. I am sweaty from dancing. It doesn't come off when I add water," Rose quipped.

"Funny."

"There, I feel a second wind. Let's do it."

"I don't know how late it is, but we may only have few chances."

The two tiptoed down the hall to the stateroom, a big room normally used for dinner parties. It looked ultra-empty this time of night. Anna analyzed the room through the lens. Rose stood in so Anna could compose the shot. Rose wandered about the big room, striking funny poses, exaggerated and dramatic for Anna to set the camera for the indoor lighting. Her thoughts meandered, replaying the nights events. The click of Anna's camera brought her back. "Here give me that camera, I'm shooting you remember.

Then they traded places and Rose took a few shots. Anna did some sultry model poses. Rose shot the serious grown-up girl who had transformed through the lens. All is illusion, Rose mused. Then she told a few jokes, Anna ignored her, kept her composure, and shot her a wise and knowing look. She's old beyond her ears, Rose knew. They played around some more.

"Let's get some in the big moon light," Rose said.

"Sure. This is fun. This gives me a great excuse to call Peter tomorrow."

"How so?"

"Like you suggested, he probably has access to a dark room somewhere."

"Now you're thinking." Rose didn't want to meet anyone that's for sure. She wanted to talk to Anna about Bernard, but this was her night. As it was, she could barely get Bernard off her mind. She couldn't help but fantasize what may have happened had Krissy not looked so forlorn and lost at the bar. At this rate Rose knew she wouldn't be able to sleep. Their voices rose in excitement, they were talking too loud again, Rose realized in retrospect. She even relapsed into giggling at one of Anna's quips.

When they burst out of the hatch onto the upper deck, they heard loud voices. Screaming irate voices. Krissy had finally lost her cool.

Rose grabbed Anna's hand and they retreated softly back to the shadows. Shoes in hand, they ran swiftly back through the halls to their cabin. They fell back on to their twin beds gasping and giggling in nervous laughter.

"Time to call it a night I think." Anna began slipping off her dress and by the time she headed in to the bathroom to wash her face, Rose was already in her slip and tucking in under the white sheets.

THAT NIGHT ROSE WATCHED THE MOON OVER WATER through the porthole for a long time. As much as her heart urged her to stay, ride the wave of opportunity to see what could unfold here, she had to face facts. The lips that spoke of almost offered promises of her long night, tugged at her heart. Dry, boring, real facts kept surfacing amidst the sweet recollections. Ah, and she believed in the fantastic.

Anna had a round-trip plane ticket, with a return date on Air France. The trouble was, how could she convince Anna it was time to leave when she herself wanted to stay? She was good at self-denial. She was good at saying no and sticking to a plan. She struggled. Was she self-sabotaging herself and her highest desire here? Or would she abandon her duty to her sister and her family? What was more important in the long run? Anna. She had to think of Anna. The conundrum morphed into a sweet dreamless sleep.

16

CONFLICT

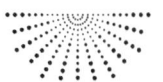

*W*hen Bernard and Rose strolled casually back on to the yacht. The lights were dim and things were quiet. Krissy sat alone at the bar crouched over her drink. It looked like just the latest one in a long line of martinis.

"Oh there you are, Bernard honey." She turned, pushed off the bar and sauntered up to them slurring a little.

"Hey. Is Anna back yet?" Rose asked.

"In her room." Krissy sniffed.

" 'Night. I will join her." Rose kept her head down as she tiptoed out in bare feet.

Krissy slipped into an armchair. "How about a night cap?" she asked Bernard.

Rose scampered down the corridor to her room feeling guilty. She rapped on their cabin door. "Anna?"

"I'm here."

As Rose entered slowly, she saw Anna looking gorgeous. She was all done up with a new hairstyle similar to her earlier swing, but fresh and daring. Her eyes looked huge, with all the layers of eye shadow and mascara.

"When did you guys get back?" Rose asked.

"Not long ago. We were at a party at La Mansione, in that arty town. Krissie is pissed because Bernard was supposed to join us. He never showed."

"He must have forgotten."

"On purpose more like. Let me look at you." She twirled Rose around to get a better look. She whistled, "Nice dress."

"It's nothing. You look amazing. So put together. You look older. Sophisticated."

"Krissie's been great to me. Look." Anna showed her an array of packages and items arrayed on the dresser.

Rose saw perfume, make-up, a purse, belts and more laid with care on the bed.

Anna was saying, "Lancôme, Channel, Cole Hahn, Juicy Couture…"

"Wow. She's gone way out."

"She charges it all."

"Was it great? The party and all?" Rose was stung at the obvious insult. "Why didn't you tell me about it. I would have reminded him, had I known."

"It's funny. I don't understand at all. But it seems when I heard them talking, she wanted Bernard to come. It was an important introduction she was making. She didn't want anything to spoil it."

"Spoil it?"

"Her big plans. I don't know. I met an absolutely fabulous Greek guy named Peter. She introduced me to so many people I can't even keep it straight. Then we came back here. I couldn't wait to see you…show you."

"Did you mean I wasn't invited to the party on

purpose?" Rose felt stung. "What's up with that? I feel bad. I'm your sister. Why do you just want to abandon me?"

"It's not me. Krissie calls the shots. I wanted to bring my bags back, pick you up, she said there wasn't time. She didn't want to be late. " Anna paced, and stopped in front of the mirror captivated by her look. "Its not on purpose or anything. I just thought Bernard would bring you, naturally."

"Oh, I see. So you think he knew all along, and didn't want to take me? Is he, are they embarrassed about me? What's so bad about me?"

"Well, you are different." She stared back at Rose over her shoulder.

"You, on the other hand, are all made up to perfection. Ah well. I'm glad I get to see you all done up. I certainly don't want to spoil your evening. So tell me about this Peter."

"OK. He's 29. Kind of old but so-oo successful. He's a photographer for Vogue and he wants to shoot me. He gets to call a lot of the shots you know, choose his subjects. The others are sent out as needed on assignment. He makes his own assignments."

"Wow, that is really awesome news. On two levels."

"Yeah? How so?"

"I bet he has a studio, and a dark room. Where is he from? Does he live around here?"

"A local? No way. This is the scene. He's here to make the scene."

"Well, give me some details then. What's he really like?"

"Longish sun-streaked hair like Gerard's. By the way Gerard likes you, he was asking where you were. Anyway, deep brown eyes. A nice accent." Anna shrugged nonchalantly. "Your type. No biggie to me. I like to listen to him talk."

"Now you sound like me."

"Dresses neat. Blue jeans, boots, a sports coat. I think he's like us. Pulled himself up. Works hard, willing to do what it takes. An artist. He looks at me like he's looking into or beyond me. I can see his wheels turning, It's odd. It's different. He likes my look. That's what counts." She shrugged.

"I get it. He sounds cool."

"I met so many people. Next time you have to come. Krissie was parading me around like a pet poodle at a show or something."

"Maybe she thinks she's inventing you. Has some sort of ownership."

"Like she got mad when I spent too much time with Peter. I don't know, jealous or something? Almost as if I was supposed to stay with her and nod and smile on demand. If I hadn't met Peter, I wouldn't have had any fun really." Anna was quiet as she thought about it. "It's like what you said about the object thing. In my mind I wanted it. To be this beauty that could make money just being me. Then when I got back here to the boat, I wanted you to see the total affect. So I couldn't relax. Look. I can barely sit down! It's funny really. I can't wash my face."

Rose jumped up. "I got it. Here, get your camera. There are some huge full-length mirrors in the stateroom. We could go in there, and you could take some self-portraits. I can take some too. You have a good eye. You can direct me. First, I need to wash my face. I am sweaty from dancing. It doesn't come off when I add water," Rose quipped.

"Funny."

"There, I feel a second wind. Let's do it."

"I don't know how late it is, but we may only have few chances."

The two tiptoed down the hall to the stateroom, a big room normally used for dinner parties. It looked ultra-empty this time of night. Anna analyzed the room through the lens. Rose stood in so Anna could compose the shot. Rose wandered about the big room, striking funny poses, exaggerated and dramatic for Anna to set the camera for the indoor lighting. Her thoughts meandered, replaying the nights events. The click of Anna's camera brought her back. "Here give me that camera, I'm shooting you remember.

Then they traded places and Rose took a few shots. Anna did some sultry model poses. Rose shot the serious grown-up girl who had transformed through the lens. All is illusion, Rose mused. Then she told a few jokes, Anna ignored her, kept her composure, and shot her a wise and knowing look. She's old beyond her ears, Rose knew. They played around some more.

"Let's get some in the big moon light," Rose said.

"Sure. This is fun. This gives me a great excuse to call Peter tomorrow."

"How so?"

"Like you suggested, he probably has access to a dark room somewhere."

"Now you're thinking." Rose didn't want to meet anyone that's for sure. She wanted to talk to Anna about Bernard, but this was her night. As it was, she could barely get Bernard off her mind. She couldn't help but fantasize what may have happened had Krissy not looked so forlorn and lost at the bar. At this rate Rose knew she wouldn't be able to sleep. Their voices rose in excitement, they were talking too loud again, Rose realized in retrospect. She even relapsed into giggling at one of Anna's quips.

When they burst out of the hatch onto the upper deck, they heard loud voices. Screaming irate voices. Krissy had finally lost her cool.

ROSE GRABBED ANNA'S HAND AND THEY RETREATED SOFTLY back to the shadows. Shoes in hand, they ran swiftly back through the halls to their cabin. They fell back on to their twin beds gasping and giggling in nervous laughter.

"Time to call it a night I think." Anna began slipping off her dress and by the time she headed in to the bathroom to wash her face, Rose was already in her slip and tucking in under the white sheets.

That night Rose watched the moon over water through the porthole for a long time. As much as her heart urged her to stay, ride the wave of opportunity to see what could unfold here, she had to face facts. The lips that spoke of almost offered promises of her long night, tugged at her heart. Dry, boring, real facts kept surfacing amidst the sweet recollections. Ah, and she believed in the fantastic.

Anna had a round-trip plane ticket, with a return date on Air France. The trouble was, how could she convince Anna it was time to leave when she herself wanted to stay? She was good at self-denial. She was good at saying no and sticking to a plan. She struggled. Was she self-sabotaging herself and her highest desire here? Or would she abandon her duty to her sister and her family? What was more important in the long run? Anna. She had to think of Anna. The conundrum morphed into a sweet dreamless sleep.

17
RIVIERA ROMANCE

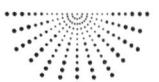

*T*he next morning, Bernard rushed through his morning's tasks. Once completed, he sought out Rose.

She, still tingly from last night's memories, had risen early and left the boat for a stroll along the boardwalk. Her heart was full. She felt she could soar with the birds, which danced along the shore. She knew Bernard's habits and went back to busy herself with tasks on the boat. She felt too anxious to concentrate on drawing. The sketches she made were rushed and abstracted partial starts.

Bernard found her alone, he watched as she tossed crusts of crumbs to the gulls. "Good day," he joined her at the rail.

Rose turned and smiled, "what's up?"

"I was wondering. Are you up for a drive?"

"Perhaps. Where did you have in mind."

I was thinking of Nimes. We haven't visited it since that daring tango on the bridge."

"Ah ha. I remember."

"I am hoping Anna and I can develop them.

"The photo shoot Krissy took Anna to resulted in quite a few good pictures of her. I hear they are soon to be published in Elle."

Rose nodded. That was good. Well done Anna she thought.

"As for. Me, I rather enjoyed the dance at the the Pont du Gard."

"Wow. That's when we first came. Seems like ages ago."

"Let's do it. It's off the beaten path and has an air of mystery about it."

"It's a fantastic place. Yes, I would like that."

Before she could ask, Bernard said, "I am borrowing Gerard's car. It's only an hours drive by auto."

SOON THE WIND IN HER HAIR, BERNARD TOOK THE TURNS fast. Smoothly winding along the coast before the turn-off up into the hills. The Alfa Romeo was smooth on the road. Bernard apparently loved to drive. Rose leaned back into the thrill of it, the sun warm on her face. She'd used a scarf to tie her curls down tight. She felt she was in a 60's film. Driving was like freedom. She watched Bernard's serious profile, his gloved hands light on the steering wheel, his eyes focused ahead. She settled back into the white leather seat. The crystal blue car matched the sky. The azure water glinted a bright sun back at her from the expanse of sea.

She saw the Pont du Gard aqueduct in the distance as they neared the small town. As they drew closer, the powerful force of the monument hit her. The 3-tiered bridge structure was both function and beauty, carrying both water and people. The ingenuity of the engineering feats that connected and united Europe to become a great empire, were truly magnificent. People often spoke of the fall of Rome. Here was a place to contemplate greatness. This ancient town was full of Roman monuments, this one might be as old as the 1st century. She stayed focused on this huge expansive structure. The last time they had been there with the group, everyone focused on their new endeavor. She trying to hold her own; act like she knew what she was doing. She really was winging it—figuring it all out as they went. She remembered; everyone had been talking at once, Krissy trying to be a star, the music blaring oldies from the boom box. Today, after they parked and walked towards the aqueduct, she felt a sense of awe, and respect. Wind blew up in gusts and her hair flew across her eyes. Her skirt whipped around her legs.

| "Pont du Gard- Aqueduct"

Bernard took her hand and they approached the place with reverence. Neither spoke as Rose took it all in. She slipped off her sandals and walked barefoot feeling the cold stone on her bare feet. Each step more careful with the rough grit between her toes. The view from up here at the chasm below was amazing. A cool breeze dusted her cheek as she gazed out over the rugged landscape. Bernard was Italian, he must be proud of his ancestors' achievements. Romans had left their mark from Greece to the British Isles. Although the fall was real, the remnants of greatness were all around Europe. What of the fall of Atlantis? Theirs was—according to Plato—a great culture. Where are those remnants? What did they look like? If there aren't any, doesn't that in itself say something?

She glanced up at Bernard who was content not to speak. She sensed they had come here for a reason. She intuited, being here was the gift. In the middle, she stopped and gazed out for a long while. She was suddenly very glad they had done the photo shoot here. She would do what she could to get them developed somewhere. Perhaps in town. Today as she concentrated on the distant view, she imprinted the scene on the retina of her memory. Then he took her hand and pulled her to him.

He held her close, and she stayed in his arms a long while. In the embrace, she felt the past and the future and the timeless present. She felt complete. She would hold this feeling in her, as they were now, poised, suspended over time. When she looked up into his face his eyes held hers with a serious gaze. Saying nothing, bridged all the language barriers between them.

When they returned to the boat, he explained, "I have the inevitable meeting in town this evening."

" The one you have been waiting for?"

"I have been dreading it. A few of the members have now arrived and we can at last get on with it. I must prepare to leave. This matter demands my complete attention. I trust you have everything you need?"

"Can I help in some way?"

"No," He smiled so warmly, "Yes, my pet, look in on Yvette, and keep my boat safe for my return."

Rose looked perplexed.

"I may stay a few nights away. These meetings are at a hotel and go very late."

"Well then, Bernard, thanks for today." She smiled sweetly, "See you later."

She headed back to her room to find her sister with a song in her heart.

LAST DAYS

*A*fter a sad day of wandering the coves and making lonely, detailed sketches, Rose was prepared for the inevitable. Unsure how long it would take to get her sister back to Paris on time, Rose decided it was time to leave.

The next morning, after a small breakfast of soft-boiled eggs and salmon toast, the two sisters went on their customary swim. Rose luxuriated in the bracing cool water. She imagined the full moon had left some magic in it. The swim was a baptism of sorts; a place to give her the courage for the next step. The water woke her up and sparked her brain. It fired with the customary excitement of possibility. She lay on the thick borrowed towel in the warmth of the sun to calm the chill and soften her goose bumps.

"Anna, are you alright?" She turned to her sister.

"I've been thinking. I think it's weird how Krissy keeps running my life. I'm pretty sure she is separating us on purpose. It concerns me about her motivations. I really insisted on picking you up the other night before the big party. She made one excuse after the other."

Wow, I missed yet another party. "What's wrong with me? I like parties," Rose said. "Frankly, it was so quiet on the boat. Everyone had disappeared. I didn't know where any one was."

"Honestly, I think they were all lies. It's some kind of control she wants over me. She doesn't know I'm my own person," Anna said. "I know soon you will have to go back to Paris and our aunt Edith. Krissy is trying to convince me to stay. How do I know it's not more lies? She's vague. Doesn't give me specifics I can check out. I honestly don't think I can handle it alone."

"Part of growing up is *knowing* yourself," Rose said. "*Knowing* what you are ready for and want."

"She's so schizo, Krissy I mean. She just jumped all over Bernard the other night. You two were both missing when we returned late from the party last week, she won't let it go. It's like she thought you were out on a date or something," Anna said. "As if. She was like a scathing serpent. But when you walked in, I bet she was all sweetness. You disappeared fast. That was smart. She had been fuming over martinis all night. I'd never seen that side of her. She was my idol for heaven's sake."

By now it was growing late and Rose and Anna were alone at the beach. The same beach where they had swum the first day they arrived. Gazing out at everyone with their striped towels and blue umbrellas.

"You might be interested in what I've been thinking," Rose said. "Your return flight. We have got to be back in Paris in time. And we must hitch a ride to get there. We've created this illusion of being so carefree and fun. Americans who forgot to make a reservation. But in truth we must bow out gracefully and hit the road once again like a pair of typical American tourists. Not like the broke vagabonds we really are."

"Correction. Photographers on a shoot," Anna chuckled. "That reminds me, I want to call that photographer guy Peter today. See if he has a darkroom around here somewhere."

"Did you hear me? Paris? Your flight?" Rose said. "We have to leave here."

"Oh. Not today surely."

"Not today, silly. I am serious, though, tomorrow. Morning at the latest. See what I mean though? It's more fun to take photo's than be in them. Be the creator of the image. Not the image."

"You should see those shots I took of you the other night in the state room – all dreamy eyed. You can't fool me. We are different there," Anna said. "But it is odd. Being paraded around like a beauty queen. It's great, all the attention. I don't know what to think. Do I have to choose?"

Rose laughed. "No. No I guess not." She didn't speak for a long while as she studied her sister. She was still propped on her side. Her head rested on her hand shading her eyes from the lowering sun. Her arm grew tired, sand in her eyelashes.

"Hey, let's grab an espresso at that beach café. We need to make a plan."

At the small café, all white stucco and blue tile, it reminded Rose of Greece. She ordered spanakopita to go with the coffee. "It's amazing how our funds hold out when someone else has been housing and feeding us night and day."

"Someone…Bernard," Anna said. "Do you think she's jealous?"

"Mm, Who?" Rose enjoyed the first sip of her latte. Foam sticking to her upper lip.

"Krissy, I thought she was just possessive of me and jealous of our closeness," Anna said. "It may be more than that. Oh well. Let's call Peter. He gave me his card." She got up to find a payphone.

"Look, if we get a good night's sleep and head out in the morning, we can get back to Paris with quite a few days to spare," Rose said. "It's a long way. If rides are slow, we may not get there in time."

"You're right." Anna sat back down. " Or I could stay here and meet this mysterious agent who knows absolutely everyone," Anna said. "And if it doesn't work out at all…"

"You will be out a flight back. And be out here on your own," Rose said. "Bernard and his Yacht are surely on the way to somewhere soon. I never pry. I get the feeling he's getting antsy about something. You certainly couldn't hitch alone. I mean, if you were determined to stay, I should stay too." Rose's eyes grew wide as she anticipated the idea. Her heart beat fast at the thought of Bernard. Right. She could use Anna as an excuse to justify some hidden desire of her own. Anna was younger. She was the adult here. "This is crazy. You know, till everything is settled."

"I see your point."

"It's not easy. Believe me, I want the best for you. You are only seventeen. You can stay in touch with Krissy, go back home and save more money, and come back with a plan." She studied Anna's face that was still as she considered her options. "You need to be more independent. Have a backup plan if it doesn't work out."

"In that case," Anna's black eyes glinted when she made up her mind, "if we absolutely have to leave these guys, there is one more adventure on my list."

Rose- took a careful bite of the flakey spanakopita, unsure what Anna would say.

"You spoke earlier about a miracle," Anna said. "I don't want to lose track of my original intentions in making the trip."

"If you are serious about praying for a miracle, then let's visit the site of all French Miracles," Rose said. "Lourdes. Where Bernadette saw our Lady."

"You read my mind. It's in France, we are in France, duh," Anna said.

"Yes. You mean you want to go to Lourdes?"

"Yes, I do. The place of Miracles and Saint Bernadette."

Rose broached the subject again.

"Of course, haven't you thought it strange that so far everyone that helped us on our journey is named Bernard?"

"I thought there was a shortage of French names."

"Funny."

"I know it's slightly off our route, but as we are on foot, a pilgrimage is totally in order. Arriving on foot, our belongings on our back, is like a real pilgrimage," Rose enthused. Smiling to appear surer of herself for her sister's sake.

"Our bags stuffed with new clothes, books, shoes, and treasures."

"True." Rose was glad Anna still had a sense of humor.

After a long stretch while both sisters pondered the reality of the road once more. Rose spoke up, "You know it's in the wrong direction?" Now Rose felt like she was losing a battle with a two-year-old. First, she convinced Anna to leave the Riviera—where everything is going like a dream—And for great valid serious reasons. Now Anna agrees but wants to go the wrong way. For a noble cause and everything.

"Oh please? I really meant what I said about our parents," Anna begged. "I could handle *home* again, with a little help."

"With a little help from our angelic friends? Blessings from above?" Rose believed in miracles.

"You have the idea." Anna smiled.

Rose breathed a sigh of relief. Anna was sensible after all. Her plane ticket was a guaranteed lifeline to jerk her back to her own reality. Good or bad. She was as scared as Rose to go out on a limb into the unknown, what-if, of empty promises. They were partners in the new illusion of moneyed success. She had dared to think she had a chance with Bernard when all it was, was a few gifts and dinner.

Perhaps miracles were in order at this point. Now she was glad Anna had agreed with the alternative. Agreeing was the first step, acting on it was the current dilemma

Rose still hadn't run into Bernard. When she spotted Javier, he only nodded and looked serious. "Bernard sends his regrets. He is still tied up with business matters."

"Is everything alright?"

"Oh yes, rest assured, Bernard always handles his business with great discretion. I'm sure all is well."

Back in her cabin, she began gathering her things and supplies. Leaving meant packing, and she went about the task with leaden arms. She made a neat pile of her many watercolors. She had propped them up around the room, a document of her progress.

PETER AT LAST

*R*ose was still dragging her feet about leaving although convinced they were both out of their element. The dynamics of Krissy and Bernard's entanglement was way beyond them. Something dark seemed to be eating at Bernard. He was preoccupied. Krissy had yet to deliver anything substantial for Anna. Her thoughts stopped mid track when Anna burst in breathless.

"I'm off again. Krissy says she will go with me to Peter's studio. I told her I wanted to meet with him. She insists I shouldn't go alone. She offered to take me."

Roses' heart fell. They had been carried away yesterday and she had never made that call. She wanted this meeting for Anna. "OK. She may be right. Shall I come with?"

"You can. I think. If you must. I don't want to deal with Krissy's complaints."

"No. You are right. I don't want to force myself."

She'd barely spoken and then Anna was gone again. Rose used to be like that—always on to the next adventure, leaving her sister Murielle in the dust. Alone. Now she was on the receiving end and had to take the medicine. It made her feel strange. Jilted? Lonely? But no, not here on such a glorious afternoon.

With mixed feelings, after she had gotten most of her and Anna's stuff organized and packed, she headed outside. This time no one was around so she took an evening stroll on the boardwalk.

She wondered about loneliness. This alone time she seemed to have a lot of had a comforting aspect to it. As she strolled and watched the birds flight and flirt with the tossing angry waves, she realized poetry was singing in her head. Words were finding their way in a rhythm with the waves. Something new, that couldn't be captured in paint and color. Something was timeless about poetry. It linked memory with the present and the unsung future of possibility. True, she was alone. Yet she felt a pending pregnant anticipation. Perhaps she was OK about leaving after all.

Anna intoned that Krissy, as she was her entre to this fashion world insisted on attending any meetings Anna might have to further her career. "It's for your own good. I must ensure your safety. One never knows about photographers."

The next morning, however, Anna complained that the meeting with Peter had been postponed until today. Instead, she'd been whisked off to a boring meeting with stogy men. Rose thought it was an opportunity. She was determined to get the Aqueduct photo shoot printed while they were still here. Her time spent on the Pont with Bernard now made that imperative. If she could only have a few prints. She wasn't even sure how much Anna had caught on camera but hoped there was at least one of her tango with Bernard. That was something she could give Bernard.

"Hey, I got almost everything packed and organized yesterday. I'm free and I would really like to meet him. I've got it, Anna. I'll come with and hang out nearby. I can keep an eye on you guys from a distance."

THUS AGREED, ANNA JOINED KRISSY TO MEET PETER AT AN outdoor cafe in town. When Rose spotted them, she dipped into a weaving store nearby. She really wanted to meet this guy too. As she didn't want to intrude, she'd figure out a way for it to seem natural. From her vantage point, Rose could see Anna, bent toward Peter in earnest conversation. Krissy leaned back in her chair and put out her cigarette, then reapplied her lipstick. She glanced around in every direction, crossed and uncrossed her legs. Anna and Peter seemed to be in their own world. Peter was serious and Anna was smiling, she laughed and the sound carried across the cobblestones. Krissy lit another and blew smoke rings. Rose started counting the seconds on her fingers, a bored Krissy wouldn't stay put long. Krissy abruptly interrupted them and excused herself. She picked up her large black bag and smiled pertly as she rose from the table. Peter must have asked to bum a cigarette because she fumbled through her purse and offered him one, then gestured towards the shops and took off, clutching her bag to her side like a security blanket. Shopping was the cure for all sorts of ills, Rose mused.

Rose took her cue and strolled by casually. "Anna," she exclaimed when she was close, "there you are."

"Let me introduce you. My sister, Rose. Peter, I don't know your last name."

"Polydorus."

"Rose, this is Peter Polydorus, the photographer Krissy was raving about."

"Pleased to meet you. Where is she, by the way, your keeper?"

"She went shopping. She can't resist the shops." Ignoring her dig, Anna waved casually towards the quaint row of shops a block away.

Peter stood and offered Rose a café.'

"Yes, thanks, sounds lovely. So glad I ran into you guys." Rose took a seat at the empty café chair, placing her backpack beside her on the ground. "Don't let me interrupt. I'm sure you too have a lot in common. Anna is quite the photographer. She works with my dad in the studio."

The two resumed their discourse. It was shoptalk beyond Rose's understanding. Darkrooms; chemicals; timing; black and white vs. color. She nodded at the waiter and ordered water and a café au lait when he approached. As she listened to the talk, she observed this French guy. He wore tight black jeans and cowboy boots. His light blue linen shirt was partly untucked and half unbuttoned with the sleeves rolled up over tan forearms. She was surprised to see a Rolex watch loose on his wrist. He wore his gold–auburn hair longish and tucked behind his ears. She was glad they were so absorbed and she could observe.

Then he turned to include Rose in the conversation. "Your sister knows quite a bit about cameras."

"Our Dad is a photographer."

"So, she says. Photography is a good game. I love it. I have been making my living with a camera for a while now." He sipped his café. "Your sister has a good look— very European—with strong features. But she is young. I took some good shots the other day. I printed a few."

"I'd love to see them."

"Sure? I have a place, not too far from here. Tucked back in the barrio section."

"When can we go?"

"Well... uoff," shrug.

Rose looked from face to face. "What about now? I mean we are here. The day's ours. Krissy?" She inquired at Anna.

"She can shop for days. It will be hours before she even remembers us."

"Sure. How far is it? Can we walk?"

"Of course, it's in the back streets by the Canal. There are fishermen's houses and some row houses near the warehouses. You've never been there I take it? It's the locals' side of town."

"Are you from here?" Rose asked.

"No. I grew up in Marseilles. I studied in Paris of course."

"Photography or Art?"

"No. Everything else. The camera was my friend. I had a knack. Paris is too formal. I prefer the south of France. It's more relaxed, casual."

Rose and Anna laugh together. "You are a beach bum."

Peter shrugged. "I make my living with my camera. I travel light."

"A rolling stone," Rose said.

"Yeah, the Stones."

"I love them."

"Me too. Finish up. Come on I'll show you the other side of town and my studio. We will listen to some cool British rock music."

"Lead on." Anna looked at Rose, they both grinned.

FRIENDS

*R*ose trailed behind. She followed them through the maze of cobblestone streets. She had never bothered to venture away from the sea. The places were older and shabbier further away from the coast. Houses were close together and only two stories. Plaster fading, brick exposed beneath, wood balconies worn with time and the sea. It had lots of character. Rose could feel the time-worn charm of this world. They passed cheese shops and the bakery. Smells of flowers and garlic mixed in with a sort of musk smell. It was pleasant.

Anna really lit up when she talked about cameras. She was so confident in this milieu. Really now that Rose thought about it, she was sort of insecure about her looks. She adopted a mysterious silence when around people and seemed stuck-up. By now Peter and she had switched cameras and were shooting each other.

Rose surmised Peter was about twenty-nine or so, definitely too old for Anna. He was a good big brother age. Finally, down another street and through a wide painted door, they entered a courtyard. There was laundry hung

on the line out the upper windows. Back against the far
end was a long flat high whitewashed brick wall with a
door. Peter opened it with a small key and they entered.
The place was dark and narrow.

It opened up toward the back to a tall, wide expanse
painted white.

"It used to be a stable," Peter explained, he was
excited, "but it's perfect." Peter was visibly proud. "If I
didn't have this place," his voice trailed off.

Really, the place was one large room of studio space.
The narrow dark space was where he ate and slept. A small
bed was cot-like against the wall, doubling as a couch.
There was a counter with an Italian espresso maker and a
small fridge. Rose took in the details, as Peter engaged
Anna totally with the ten or so 8x10's he had clipped to a
line outside his darkroom. "I want to see." Rose ran to
catch up.

She stopped and took in the photos. Peter stopped
talking while the sisters studied his work. They were black
and white and they were all of Anna. Cool cropped close-
ups. Moody eyes, nose, and mouth. Cheekbone silhouetted
against a stormy sky. Rose thought it was almost abstract in
a way.

"This is art," Rose said.

"Yes." Peter nodded with his eyes. He knew she got it.
"This is not what I showed Krissy. I gave her what she
asked for. This is work I keep for myself."

Anna was quiet. She nodded her head.

"Let's have some wine." Peter was suddenly the gregar-
ious host. He went to the small fridge and grabbed a
chilled bottle of white wine and small glasses. He poured
one for each and got another for himself. They sat at a
small table in the otherwise empty big room.

"My studio. Fantastic yeah?"

It wasn't empty really. There were photo poles and lights and all kinds of studio stuff. But it was bare. Austere.

"We feel at home here," Anna laughed. "Don't we Rose?"

"Yes. Our Dad's place looked like this."

"I do commercial shoots. I work with models, do their portfolios. I submit to a few, a lot, of magazines, Elle, Vogue, Italy and France." He shrugged. "I'm hired for shoots. It's a hustle. But some work is for me. Did Krissy say I wanted to meet you?"

"No. We wanted to meet you!" Anna said. "True story, we have an agenda."

"We did a photoshoot last week right after we first arrived. We were on a roll, taking photos of everyone we met along the way on our travels," Anna said.

Rose was excited now. "I love dance, and I have this theory about dance. Choreographers can't do their work without a stage and an audience, such a production. And as I am a bit of a vagabond—or a gypsy—I love to travel. I want to be on the move, exploring. I always thought if you could create a dance on-site, a great site, and just film it or photograph it, the dance could still tell the story. But more as a series of stills shots. You could still have the joy of dancing it, of course. I guess it's like performance art. Site-specific."

Subsequently, we designed a dance shoot, complete with costumes, for fun, with all those we had met on the boat. Krissy, Bernard, and the gang were the dancers. Anna shot several rolls of film."

"We usually send everything back to Dad to develop. He gets a record of our trip in the process."

"We held on to these. I thought if we could find a darkroom, we could develop them ourselves. Have creative control." Rose caught her breath. "You see, Anna wants to be a model, but I think she's great behind the camera."

Peter's eyes widened as they tracked from left to right between the two sisters, watching the girl's animated discourse. Both were talking at once. "Wait. Stop." He held his hand out, palm up. "Rose, I can see you really care a lot about this. First, one at a time. Both are good professions and both are difficult. Now, Anna. Miss Anna, why do you want to be a model?" he stuck a mock microphone to her mouth for her reply.

"Simple. Money. I want to be rich."

He stopped open-mouthed; He had never heard that from one so young. "Sure, it's possible. I don't think that's good enough. Give me more. I'm listening."

"I love fashion. I love clothes, and design. And money, and 'the look'. I believe I know how to have it. 'All that.' What sells. I'm smart. And complex. I have both sides, creative and shrewd. I know what I want. I want to go and get it. For instance, Rose.

"She is three years older than I am. She goes to university. She's good, makes straight A's, knows her stuff. She's accepted into Art School and Architecture school at UT Austin. After three years of academia, she's less sure, less confident. More obedient. It's like she's been watered down. Grades are like a judgment. Then to make the good grades she compromises her vision and her herself.

"She's already an Artist. She already has vision. In High School, she had shows of her unique work in fiber arts. Then a bunch of wannabe artists at university—academicians, begin to judge her, and grade her, compare her. She compares herself. Now she's stressed from school— broke—because she spends all her money on school. After three years I don't know if she will ever get a job. And then the problem is –it's a job! And now, actually, so confused, she took off to Europe and has been bumming around for three months with no plans to return.

"On the other hand, modeling is fun! It's fashion, and adventure, and travel."

Rose chimed in,-"Starvation."

Peter's arms were crossed as he leaned back taking it all in. "It looks fun. That's an illusion. It's hard work if you can get it. Then it's hard to keep getting it. Auditioning is an unpaid job. Traveling is grueling hours and deadlines, with no time to bask in the sun or stroll by the sea. Unless it's part of the shoot. And it's a hustle. A damn hustle. You must have perseverance. It's full of rejection, and self-esteem problems. Which often leads to drug issues, just to cope. Fashion changes like underwear. What's cover material today, takes out the trash tomorrow.

"Easy to string you along while you are young and hot. Beauty fades. When yours does, you're out.

"Not you, mind you. I am not speaking personally, but just a general overview. There is always an exception to every rule. You're young, but you're old too. I can see you're smart. You know your cameras and your angles. But the answer I was looking for...Hey what about Photography?"

"I love it," Anna said simply.

Everyone fell silent. Those words sure and clear, hung in the blue air.

"I love it,"

Anna sipped her wine. Rose smiled and twirled the bronze liquid in the glass. Peter grinned and snapped a photo of the two sisters.

"About those rolls of film, do you happen to have them with you?" Peter broke the silence. " If you do, I will develop them. While they're drying, we can all go out for an early supper. I know a great Mediterranean place near here.

"I thought you were French?"

"My mother's French. But with a name like Polydofus, my Dad's Greek."

Yes, he had that Greek sailor look about him. His coloring was French, with reddish auburn curls, and gold skin. They were part Greek, she was sure, mixed in with all that French. Anna poured over Peter's photo's while he was busy in his darkroom developing the film. He had stacks of 8x 10's, both black and white, and color, laying about, and a pile of contact sheets.

After a long dinner filled with side dishes of spanako-pita, olives, hummus, and pita, they went back to Peter's and stayed late printing photographs. At the end of the evening, Peter escorted them both back to the boat.

Her thoughts turned back to Bernard. She'd hardly seen him the last few days. Only a brief glimpse either coming or going. Something really preoccupied him. There was so much she didn't know. She was definitely afraid to ask.

'Follow your passion', Rose repeated in her mind. That is always the answer. Much later, as the boat rocked her to sleep, she drifted off wondering what was *her* passion?

21

PETER'S STUDIO

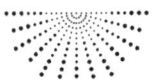

*J*ust as she was sure the right-responsible thing to do was to leave, get Anna back home, she was completely unsure. Rose was beginning to really like Bernard and Peter was giving Anna a break from all Krissy, all the time. Anna was now all about Peter and his darkroom and his amazing camera and lenses. They had barely gotten any sleep after the long day and dinner they had spent together. After a quick breakfast and a morning swim, they both were on their way to the other side of town to visit Peter's studio once again. They were eager to see the photo's they'd chosen to print. They had left them on the line to dry the day before. Peter had offered, time allowing, to print a few more that morning.

When he opened the door, he welcomed them with a big grin. "You've great timing. I just put the coffee on." The smell of espresso infused the small kitchenette as the Italian stovetop espresso maker bubbled. He poured them each espresso in porcelain cups. "Milk? Sugar?" He opened the small fridge and sniffed the milk carton.

"Yes , please." Rose took the carton.

"Black is fine," Anna said and blew on her cup.

As Rose watched Anna study the prints with a prac-
ticed eye, she realized they were both a bit windblown.
They'd come straight from the swim. Anna had let the sun
dry her hair and she was now her natural self. They were
both more like the day they had arrived, only with deeper
tans. Anna's hair had red highlights and her nose showed a
few freckles. Her lips were full and her deep brown eyes
looked big still outlined in waterproof mascara. She's not
self-conscious when she's focused, Rose noticed. I guess we
are all a bit like that.

Peter spoke, "The contact sheets show the sequence of
the dance shots." He gestured to a few he'd check marked.
"I selected a few from each row and the photos tell the
story. Yet it doesn't matter at all. The shots are interesting.
Many work as a stand-alone. These show Rose dancing
with a guy in black. Looks like a tango."

Rose glanced over. She opened her eyes in surprise.
Bernard and she were off to the side of the group and
Anna had caught them. In some they were mere silhou-
ettes in the distance, and some she zoomed up on. Her face
was calm, serious, pensive.

Peter glanced at Rose. "That's you. Quite the mysterious one, lost in the shadows. Or not so lost after all? Eh?"

Rose blushed. This shed a new light on things. Was
Bernard in his black cape the villain? The puppet master?
He had gazed at her with an unreadable intensity.

"It's hard to keep perspective when you are
caught up."

"Anna you're good. You caught Rose, yet I noticed
she's usually off in the distance working with the dancers."

Rose was glad she didn't want to model. Her face was
too round and plain. Just an oval with eyes and a mouth,
no drama. She was glad she hadn't realized she was in the

picture. She always freezes up. They selected twelve, black and white 8x10's and hung them up with clips on the line.

"I've been in the darkroom all morning. I don't know about you, but I'm famished."

"Famished," Anna imitated his accent.

"How about diner?"

"I could eat," Rose said. "What do you have in mind?"

"Great. Pasta. I have some shrimp and I can make shrimp pasta with a tomato cream sauce right here. Pasta and wine? Sound good for you ladies?"

"Ah, and he can cook too," Rose said. "No wonder Krissy didn't want us to hang out with you alone."

"Comme Sa?"

"You know, *come back to my studio, I will show you photos and cook you dinner*. It sounds seductive."

"Ah, no. You are my friends. What do you take me for? This is good work. We are colleagues."

"Yeah, it's true," Rose said.

Anna poked her head in the fridge. "And cucumbers. We can make a cucumber salad with feta cheese."

Rose gazed longingly out the one large window at the sunshine. "Can we eat outside?"

"Of course, Bien sur."

They all bumped into each other in the tiny kitchen while they made lunch. This was so normal and fun. Yet, the detail of Peter's watch nagged at her. A Rolex? It made him seem like a playboy or something. She dropped her worries and together they carried a small bistro table outside to the big sunny courtyard. The smell of garlic hung in the air. Peter tossed the pasta in a large bowl with a spoon. The shrimp from the sea was plump and fresh caught. The tomatoes were sweet and garden fresh too. Anna carried the salad and rose grabbed a pile of mismatched plates from the one cupboard. As they ate and toasted and drank wine Rose knew she didn't know what tomorrow may bring but she would enjoy today.

"I loved meeting you and our time together. We must head back to Paris so Anna can catch her return flight back to Texas. Krissy has been trying to entice Anna to stay but we must go back."

"Krissy has made a lot of promises about intros to agents. We have yet to see if anything comes of it."

"Krissy does tend to over-extend herself." Peter said, "But really the choice, options are all up to you." He turned to Anna. "You can't live Krissy's dream. In the meantime, photography is a real profession and you are so far ahead of the game in what you know already." He turned to Rose, "And you Rose. I like your dance moves."

"Thanks, I love to dance."

"You both are headed back to Texas?"

"Eventually, but me, not just yet. I'm staying with my aunt in Paris. I'll give you the address. Look me up if you are in town later in the fall."

"Paris is expensive."

"This place is expensive."

"For tourists yes. But here, my little place, not so much."

"You have everything you need."

As Rose sipped her wine after the giant plate of pasta was consumed, leaning back in her metal chair, she felt good. So relaxed. The laundry on the line caught the sun like a billowing sail against the blue sky. She leaned her head back far. The sun warmed her arms and her eyelids. Simple things. Like the herbs that grew in large pots in the courtyard made simple life here sweet. Rose felt grateful that Rolex or not, Peter had shared what he had with them. Rose opened her eyes. Peter was smoking a gauloise as he flipped through some Elle's and Vogue's to show Anna his published photos.

"How much do you make from these shots?"

She whistled when he told her. "So, what about these?" She gestured to their efforts.

"Yes. You can try to sell them to a magazine. Or use it in your portfolio to get new work."

"Wow. Hmm."

"I feel so peaceful and content here. You have a wonderful life. I do wish we didn't have to leave so soon. Now that we have all become friends."

"I am sorry too."

Rose began clearing up while the two were talking. She went back and forth just catching snippets of their conversation. They all carried the tables and chairs back inside together.

Peter scrawled his numbers on his business cards and gave one to each. "You are welcome back any time. Let me walk part way with you. It's a good time for a stroll through town."

"We are on our way to a miracle."

"Tell me about it next we meet."

All Rose could think to say was, "Thanks for everything, and see you later!"

That's how traveling always was at the end. Anna had taken a few photos of them all together. She had the 8x10 prints in a portfolio and all the negatives safely tucked in her camera bag. Peter headed into a shop and they sauntered back to the boat in a moody reverie.

Now, on board the yacht, the place was eerily quiet. That was a good thing, Rose decided. She was not in the mood for any more interactions. But yes, she would leave a photo of the two of them dancing for Bernard in the morning. She finished packing in silence.

After the whole day into evening off boat with Anna and their new friend Peter, Rose felt like they were a team again. The new photos were like gifts. She slipped one under Bernard's door, early in the morning the day they left for good. She kept one for herself. It was both a memory and a promise.

22

RIVIERA GOODBYE

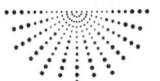

The sisters boarded a bus to the town of St. Martins, only a few days after the momentous decision to leave, putting them well on the road to Lourdes. Their leaving had been uneventful. Rose was relieved that she hadn't a chance to say goodbye to Bernard in person. He'd gone out late in the afternoon last night and hadn't returned. Their bus left early in the morning to give them a good start on the trip. Rose delayed leaving to the very last moment and nearly missed it.

Once they were beyond the streets of the village, Anna looked eager for the next phase of the journey. She had the cook pack them a bag lunch. They snacked on boiled eggs and cheeses as they rode the bus in silence. Rose's face stuck in a permanent frown was not attractive. Anna noticed but kept her own council. Who was saving whom on this venture? Anna disapproved of Roses' over friendliness with men in general. She felt the world a stage and she preferred keeping a polite distance. Rose knew this about her sister, but in her emotional state she couldn't bolster a jolly manner.

. . .

THE LONE DRIVER OF A BRIGHT BLUE RENAULT, A REGULAR guy in khaki's and a clean white knit shirt, offered them a ride. Rose explained their goal was Lourdes before nightfall.

He offered to take them all the way. When they made introductions, he too was named Bernard.

Rose gave Anna a look. She grinned and went along with it. *I guess we are on schedule after all,* Rose thought, *despite the very long completely decadent stay at the Riviera.*

"It's only a few miles past where I'm headed. I admire you girls for making the trip," Bernard said.

"I would love to hear the locals take on it." Pleased to find he spoke English so well, Rose opened the door for a story.

"Well, if you insist, I can fill you in on the local version." Bernard then spoke simply.

"She was a poor girl. Her parents worked hard, but still had little money. One frigid winter's day, Bernadette went out to gather wood to keep her family warm. She had to search far away from her home deep into a wood near a grotto. While there, Mother Mary appeared to her. She became aware of the Lady, although no one else could see her. She was told to visit regularly and do as she asked. Bernadette promised to do this.

Mary commanded Bernadette to get water from a stream, and drink from it. There was no spring. Yet, Bernadette fell to her knees and tore at the grass with her fingers until she reached mud. Her hands kept tearing at the dirt until a trickle of water came from the earth and moistened it. She grasped the fresh mud with her hands. Finally, she cupped the new water in her hands and drank.

Later, a blind man who had heard of the visions and

the new trickle of a stream, felt a ray of hope for his own ailment. He longed to see the Virgin. One night, his eyes were in such pain he thought to head out to the sacred place in the grotto. He placed the mud-water mixture on his eyes. His vision was restored and he proclaimed the miracle. Having witnessed the transformation of the blind man, many believed. A group of villagers went out with shovels and pics to dig out the place until the water ran free. This was the beginning of the sacred healing waters." When he finished he shrugged.

"That is how it all started." He looked over studying Anna intently. "Are you afflicted in some way?"

"Huh? Us? No. We're healthy," Anna said.

"Are you seeking a miracle?"

"Aren't we all," Anna quipped. The perfect scenery slipped past in silence. Anna sighed a long held breath. "It's our parents."

"They seem to be headed for disaster," Rose said. "First they got a divorce—which is bad, against our religious belief's. But then, as our mom doesn't believe in divorce, she insisted on getting an annulment."

"I want them to get back together," Anna said. "The Catholic Church granted her annulment. That makes us bastards. All nine of us."

"Nine kids?" Bernard whistled. He glanced at Anna in the rearview.

"And an annulment. Dad says it's the only sure form of birth control. Not the annulment, the divorce."

"He was joking," Rose said. "It's all my fault."

Bernard glanced at her. For a minute he seemed not to know what to say. "It is huh?"

"I'm the oldest," Rose said. "Dad and Mom kept fighting all the time. I babysat and made dinners on nights when they went to the marriage counselor. Dad kept asking me if I thought they should get a divorce since Mom wanted one so badly."

"In her mind," Anna interjected.

"Right," Rose said. "You see it's all my fault. I said 'he should' and they did. Next thing you know, it was all legal. Nine kids and child support. Each time one of us turns 18 he pays Mom less money. Of course the cost of living doesn't get any cheaper for my Mom. So when I turned 18, I was out of the house. I was cut off by default and had to pay my own way to college. Last year Murielle left to live with her boyfriend. Next year, Anna will be out on her own as well."

"Yet the bills don't get any smaller for my Mom. It's still the same size house payment, bills, insurance, food. And the boys are getting older, they eat way more than any of us girls do."

"I just want them to get back together," Anna said. "Dad loves Mom."

"Yes, he talks about her all the time. I think he thought if he did what she wanted…" Rose left the sentence unfinished, hanging. She stayed silent digesting that. It was true. He always said it. "I love no one but your Mother. Amelia Rose is my true love. She doesn't believe me. I want you girls to know. I love your Mother."

Bernard glanced at Rose, who shrugged speechless. Then in the rear view at Anna.

Adventure was a kind of high, Rose thought. Yellow lines on the Hi-way were mesmerizing. One could get addicted to motion. Just keep on keeping on, and don't look back. That's why Rose took to the road. Leaving was her 'go to.'

"I don't know what to say. Miracles are granted in Lourdes," Bernard said. "Tons of healings occur each year. If your heart is sincere…"

Anna nodded. Her dark eyes looked pained and tired. Rose wondered again what was going on in that serious head of hers. Rose marveled at Anna's innocent trust as she spilled her guts like a child to this stranger. She realized that her acting so self-assured on the yacht had left her exhausted. Such performances take their toll, she knew all too well. Acting older to feel older. Smiling to hide your sorrow until your sorrow melts into your smile. It was the same thing. Yet, it was exhausting. She could tell both of them found a new solace on the road, happy to let their hair down and be helpless hippies traveling on the whims of fate once again.

"You know, I am glad we both got to meet Peter," Rose said before they lapsed into silence.

The miles rolled by. The two girls pondered the truth of life back home. The world they had conveniently forgotten while they had been focused on survival or the next adventure.

"How long is it to Lourdes from here?" Rose broke the hush that had settled over the car like a soft blanket.

"About 400 kilometers now," Bernard said. "Not too long, about 3 hours. You like French music?" He leaned in and turned up the dial. The song—an instrumental guitar piece from Black Orpheus, came on. "Orpheus and Eurydice," he said.

"I thought that was a Brazilian film?" Rose's mind raced, wow, 3 hours in the wrong direction.

"Oh yes, filmed in Brazil but with a famous French director, Marcel Camus."

Rose smiled and nodded. She loved all things French. French films, French Jazz, French–Brazilian songs apparently. It was America she was trying to get away from.

.   .   .

SHE REPLAYED THE DISCLOSURE ANNA HAD MADE TO HER
the last night on the boat, in her mind. Rose hadn't wanted
to sleep. So the two had gone top deck and found the place
to themselves at that hour. A new friend of Krissie's had
shown up, a renowned gambler who had lured everyone
downstairs on the lower deck for cards. Thank god,
thought Rose, his cologne was killing her. She wanted fresh
air. Cards had proved addicting to the entire party. Rose
didn't know where Bernard was. He had excused himself
saying he had colleagues to meet for dinner. She hadn't
seen him return.

Anna was shivering. She seemed to have acquired a
chill. Rose found some warm blankets and covered her
from the breeze that blew up from the sea. "You know how
you went to parties with Dad's friends? All the time? When
he and Mom were separated?"

"Yes." Rose remembered. It's how she had come to
know Tim Zilco and David Watson. And various other
friends from the European club her Dad belonged to. Her
Dad's life was full of parties.

Anna continued, "Well, Mom was unavailable, so he
took you to all his events. Murielle still won't give him the
time of day. She is so mad at him about the divorce. I go
and help out at his Photography studio, in the dark room.
I'm good at developing and he is teaching me a lot. Only
now that you've left, he wants to take me to all of the
parties. I'm only 17! I'm not interested and it's not right. It
hurt his feelings that I don't like his friends. I just can't do
it. Plus I can't just stroll in to clubs like you could, acting as
if you were all old and sophisticated. Besides I don't want
to. Mom and Dad need to get back together and be proper
parents like they used to be."

Rose nodded. She remembered the dinner parties her folks had with so many interesting guests. Her Mom loved proper dinners like her days from Rosary College in Chicago with fresh rolls and place cards. When in college, she'd been the lead singer starring in all the musicals. She had tons of friends.

Of late, her Dad's photography work had opened doors in the film community. With her Mom teaching college English, there was no end to interesting visitors and guests in their home. Houston was a grass-roots place as far as the arts were concerned and the energy in the arts was amazing. As kids, they all ate first and then Rose took everyone upstairs for baths and bedtime, while the adult dinner and conversation went on for hours.

Even when they didn't have guests, her parents had often talked and discussed things at the dinner table long into the evening. They were both philosophers. Talking-discussing- debating was life-blood for them. She was glad Anna remembered and cherished those days.

"You know it was meeting Dads friend Tino and his Norwegian wife that inspired me to study art. She invited me to her studio to pose for her. Watching her paint was a lesson it itself. If I hadn't been exposed to that world...." Rose voice drifted off as she reminisced.

As Anna spoke about those days in her life, Rose knew she had her own motives for hanging out at the parties with her Dad. Home was so insular. She had so many duties and responsibilities. She hadn't made any friends her own age. She seldom had time to just hang-out. Her Dad's parties had been an entry into an adult world she was eager to join. All she had to do was listen and she learned a lot. Listen, smile, and get folks to talk if they asked her anything. She'd only been 16 and 17 then. The down side was, once she was in college and had fellow peers to hang with, they all seemed so young —and innocent. Their talk naïve and boring compared to all her Dad's friends. Also, she never had to worry, or be mistaken for available. Her Dad was her protector. That's how he'd seen it. Anna saw it differently. When Rose flirted with Gerard and Ben, it was just an easy game.

Was she just using people? She thought suddenly. Oh well, those days were over. Anna wasn't into games, or flirting.

People have different wants and needs. She looked across at the elegant package of trim elegance and perfect hair, that was Anna, sitting there, wrapped in the blanket in the moonlight. It's funny how you could be on a Yacht, surrounded by elegance, looking elegant on the outside. But inside, where it counts, all your fears and wants, desires and inadequacies were still wrapped tight and carried within.

Inside that head of Anna's was a whole world of emotions, thoughts, desires, hopes, and dreams. People were really like icebergs. Just the frosty tip showing. A whole volcano of emotion might be lurking inside— waiting just beneath the surface to erupt. She should have studied psychology, Rose thought. The art of cracking the skull of persona and perception. Wow. Perhaps being an artist was so superficial. She herself must be superficial. She sought beauty. Surrounded herself with beauty. When Krissie's serpent fangs began to show, she'd wanted to run —not confront anything—before the carriage changed into a pumpkin at midnight.

She remembered how she craved all of the parties and events she was able to attend while she was still in High school. Instead she said, "Things change. I don't know what went wrong or when."

"They can be made right. We have to have a miracle," Anna said.

Rose watched her face in the silence that hung in the air.

"That's why I came," Anna said quietly.

"Finally! Whew, I have been asking. So you do have ulterior motives."

"I'm not you. I can't go to parties with Dad like that. It's not right. It doesn't feel right."

"You don't have to either. I get it. You're all business," Rose said too harshly.

Rose remembered those dinner parties with her dad after the divorce. It seemed normal. She was glad to be included. She'd learned so much about the world that way. Her Dad had just turned forty; his friends were in their early thirties. Young professionals. This was the lifestyle he was trying to keep up with. These guys were single or pre-kids. All they had was money and time after work for parties and fun.

In reality, he had nine kids. And he lived all alone in a small apartment. Rose visited at least three times a week. And now Anna was working with him at the photography studio. It was an escape valve, she realized. Home was so insular. So cut off. They weren't even allowed to watch television.

Now her Mom had left the old neighborhood and moved to Sharpestown. Well. Rose felt she had no home now. Paris suited her just fine. But in the end, although it was in the wrong direction, Rose decided the trip to Lourdes was vital. Perhaps, she hoped, even life changing.

ANNA STIRRED ON THE BACK SEAT. ROSE LOOKED OVER AT her and smiled. Anna turned her head using her duffel as a pillow. Sweet girl, Rose thought, she had a lot on her shoulders.

That's it. She wants me back. Or she wants dad back at home. Instead, we are all trying to run away. God she was so like her father.

"Penny for your thoughts?" New Bernard asked.

"I am hoping for that miracle you mentioned," Rose said. "Have you been there?"

Bernard studied her for a minute. "Oh yes. I have made the trip many times. We'll be there in about twenty minutes."

Rose smiled her thanks and jostled Anna's leg a bit. "Anna it's time to wake up."

Anna's hair hid her face and she opened her deep brown, almond shaped eyes slowly.

Rose handed her a water bottle. "Take a sip, it will revive you." Anna seemed quite groggy. I hope I am not so naïve and she's not up to something beyond me. I should ask but I am not sure I want to know. That is cowardly.

23

LOURDES

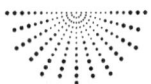

*T*he Renault crawled through the traffic on the crowded street. Rose could barely make out their surroundings through the lines of busses pulling up to hotels. On top of that, it was raining. New Bernard pulled the auto up to a hotel with a canopy so they could get out without getting completely soaked. His eyes filled with compassion when they exchanged goodbyes. Funny what you could tell a stranger. When she offered to pray for him, she had no idea what awaited them in Lourdes; this small overcrowded town at the foothills of the Pyrenees.

They waited out the sudden downpour under the jutting hotel canopy. The air felt muggy after the rain stopped. Moisture still clung in the air. This was quite a contrast to their arrival in Nice. Her eyes were heavy as she lugged her body and her bags up the cobblestone street to find a hotel for the night. All the hotels were uphill from where they were. She owed her fatigue to the late night. Her thoughts weighed her down.

She was guilty. She advised her Dad to get a divorce.

And he had. Then she ran off to college to meet her destiny, and there were eight kids left at home alone with one Mom who worked full time. Her Mom couldn't even afford to pay the bills as a teacher—her profession. So she had since quit, and had taken on all kinds of other jobs— insurance; real estate; court reporting. Things she'd hoped would pay more. Instead the family remained perpetually broke, while Mom went to jobs she disliked. Dad was severely depressed in his alone state, and his income fell as he lost good clients and his liquor consumption went up.

What could she do? A twenty-year old in Europe. What should she do? '*Stay here,*' a voice whispered in her head like a drone. Make your own life. Invent yourself.

She had taken herself as far away as she could go. She was focused on her dreams. She hadn't even glanced back. Doubt. Second-guessing: guilt. These new thoughts made her very uncomfortable.

Now what?

Rose still thought of the Riviera, and Bernard. Can two worlds that were so foreign collide? Collide and crash more like. He'd kept a professional distance for the most part. Accept those few times they had been alone together.There was that one solo afternoon with promise. She felt she *got* him though, older than she, as he was. She just understood him. He wasn't like his so called friends. He had a depth and intelligence, they seemed to lack, in her estimation. She'd caught him looking at her a time or two. They were always in crowds and groups and rarely had time alone.

He was above those theatrics Krissie and her crowd devoured. It's like—that was it—she devoured life and people too. She consumed like a fire. Yet, he'd tagged along in observer mode, the afternoon of the Roman photo shoot. Now she had proof in a photograph.

꩜

AND THEN HE'D STOOD IN FOR A TASTY ROLE AS VILLAIN—
just because she'd asked him to. Her heart zinged at the
thought. When he had looked at her with his blue eyes her
palms felt it. Her stomach dropped. But why? Why was she
so taken with such an unlikely bourgeois guy...man.

Can an escape into the arms of a wealthy handsome
man solve her problems? Here we are on earth. All of our
inner worlds held tight under lock and key, wrapped up in
beautiful packages of youth and sun and smiles. Perhaps
being a psychic would be better than being a psychologist.
People might just lie. With Bernard she liked what she saw,
but what was he hiding? She'd talked about herself too
much she realized. She'd asked about his work, his career,
and livelihood. His answers had been charming and vague,
'More wine, mon cherie?' he would say and distract her.

SHE HAD WATCHED ANNA RIDE THE WAVE OF OPPORTUNITY,
until it was absolutely time to leave the Riviera. She didn't
want her sister to be hurt. She was waiting for her to open
her eyes and see for herself. What she'd seen was Rose as
the *big* example. Things are hard at home, so leave. Take a
trip. Run away. She laughed at the parallel; Anna wanted
to use the *Runway*- as the place to run-away to. Professional
modeling was a good plan. Use what you've got. She was
young, tall, and exotic looking. All other forms of income
were delayed gratification. Get an education so you can
make money later. Modeling was a get rich now scheme.
Anna could do fall back later. When she was older and
rich. This had been difficult for Rose to see because her
values were so different. Rose thought she had set a good
example; don't smoke or drink like Dad, save money and

go to college. But she'd also gone to Europe, and that was the only part her sister seemed to pick up on. Ironically, Anna both smoked and drank just like Dad, she was on a continuous diet, just like Mom, and now she'd run off to Europe, just like her.

LOURDES WAS A SMALL TOWN PACKED WITH BIG HOTELS. Balconies hung out over the narrow cobblestoned, crowd thronged, streets. New Bernard had told them Saint Bernadette's house was just outside the village. The crowd soon became a wave pushing them away from town. There were lines everywhere, into stores, into restaurants. The heat and dust and noise of so many tourists repelled Rose. Rose looked up and out towards the mountains. She ducked into an old hotel and asked the concierge directions. The woman waved her arms and described a short walk away from the chaos. Rose smiled her thanks, *"Merci, Madame."* She and Anna crossed the square and headed away from the noise. Lucky for them, the mountain shower had stopped. The sun came out and chased away the rain clouds, leaving billowy pillows in the sky.

NO WONDER ROSE HADN'T SPOTTED SAINT BERNADETTE'S house until they wound their way up hill. There it sat, hidden behind the huge hospital. Luckily it was up hill from the rambling collection of buildings that composed the hospital. Despite the crowds that thronged the street, and the bustle that surrounded the hospital, when they finally ,climbed up through a grassy meadow to the small stone cottage that was the private home of Saint Bernadette, no one was there. There was a large chimney and a stone terrace with a wall overgrown with flowering jasmine vines. From up there, the two girls had solitude and respite in the cool mountain air. They could barely see the famous Grotto far below where Saint Bernadette's visions had occurred.

SAINT BERNADETTES HOUSE

| 'Saint Bernadette'

"This is Saint Bernadette's home. Surely she could hear our prayers here."

"I always feel that God is closer in the mountains," Rose said.

"Me too."

From their perch they watched the throngs and lines that began early and lasted all day. As the sun lowered behind the mountains, twilight claimed the day. A line of people paraded through the grotto holding lit tapers. The line snaked its way along the stream. Somehow, as they watched the show from their perch, they were not inspired to join it. Here they had come all this way for a miracle, yet, they were loath to go about asking for one.

"I just realized it's Sunday. We should go to Mass." Just then the church bells rang from down in the village. Neither girl was ready to move. Peace settled on Rose like a comforting hand she could almost feel in the warm breeze.

"You know that hospital smells horrible," Anna said.

"I guess it's all of the sick people," Rose said. "But it's like bad water and sewage. I'm afraid to go near the place with it's noxious smell everywhere."

"I like it up here."

"My thoughts exactly."

The girls pulled out a picnic of leftovers they'd scavenged from the hotel and saved from the yacht. Anna had some grapes wrapped in a cloth napkin. Rose pulled out a rather crushed white bakery bag in which she had saved some croissants. A bird sat on the sharp edge of a craggy rock and tilted its head at them. Rose studied it as she leaned back breathing in the scent of wildflowers that were strewn across the soft grass carpeted hill. She popped a few of the purple grapes in her mouth and savored the taste. Her stomach growled at the prospect of food.

The stone house wasn't open to the public, as no one was around, they could enjoy the meadow just above it. Rose thought Lourdes, over all, was strange. Up here where Saint Bernadette had dreamed and prayed was pure and natural. It was above the crowds of tourists and merchants who bought and sold miracles. Below, the crowds of tourists swarmed the streets. The shops were filled, floor to ceiling, with plastic crosses and statues of Mother Mary mixed in with reproductions of the Eiffel tower. When she glanced at the piles of cheap reproductions of plastic angels and sacred hearts, it turned her stomach. Yet people lined up everywhere to purchase the trinkets.

While they ate Anna said, "Tell me about her again."

"Bernadette was a young, fourteen year old farm-shepherdess, who spent her days in the fields. She and her three friends went to the spring for water. Mother Mary appeared to them in a vision. She fell on her knees and began to pray when the ecstatic vision befell her. Her eyes would roll up in her head and she crashed down on her knees and walk toward the vision still on her knees, stone biting into her flesh. She couldn't even feel it."

"You sound like you've seen it."

Vision continued... 4-18-17

"Well, Lourdes was the first beatific vision of Mother Mary," Rose said. "Later there were appearances in Fatima and Yugoslavia. I saw a movie they filmed of the visions in Medjugorje, Yugoslavia. Again, it was humble peasant children whom she appeared to. The messages that came through from Mary were messages—prophecies rather—about wars and the wrath of God. She always asked that mankind devote themselves to praying the Rosary for Peace—for souls, for conversion. She always spoke to humble children because, I assume, that they would listen, pay attention. She asked for a church to be built in her honor at the site of her appearances. I heard

Saint Bernadette was told a secret, and was instructed to tell only the Pope. The Pope would tell everyone when the time was at hand. The message is held in a secret trust and handed down from Pope to Pope. Until we near the day of the sign."

"The sign?" Anna was curious.

"The sun spinning in the sky, or something."

"Do you believe it?"

"Of course. I'm Catholic aren't I? I love the thought of mystery and miracles. Life without miracles? Don't know if I can go there."

"I see what you mean." Anna straightened her scapula as she spoke.

Rose fingered the small gold cross at her throat. There was a star sapphire in the center.

"I swear its glowing Rose. What did you do?"

Rose just smiled.

Now, as she sat here watching the robin, she breathed in the fresh meadow grasses, filling her lungs with sunshine. She watched as Anna took their last bit of food, two croissants, and announced 'bread-basket belly.' She tore up the bread into small pieces and tossed them to the wind. Their great grandmother had a lot of sayings passed down through the family from their Mother. One was; *you are only as young as your spine is supple.* The other one was; *you can cure most everything with apple cider vinegar and honey.* And *bread goes in the breadbasket* and pointed to your tummy. Thus, all the girls in the family were avid exercise enthusiasts, everything from weight lifting, to yoga, to dancing. Pitchers of apple cider vinegar and honey were premixed in the fridge like some people had iced tea, and there was a universal fear of bread. Anna was taking this to an extreme, Rose could see. It didn't matter that they didn't know where their next meal was coming from.

Reluctantly, the two headed down the hillside and back into town. Nothing in the whole escapade seemed sacred. How can you even find a miracle in this pile of junk? Let alone a place to sleep. No one on the streets or shops was friendly. It was a small town, with a hardened, distrustful attitude. Rose and Anna hunted for a new place to sleep. Eventually, Rose returned to the older hotel they had passed earlier. It had a view of the mountains.

She walked past the sidewalk café of tables and chairs, but few patrons. She dropped her pack off her sore shoulders, for a brief respite. Taking her sketchbook with her, she entered the dim, dark paneled, old world interior. She slipped past the main lobby and into a huge dining room crowded with tables covered in white tablecloths. She noticed peach and apple tarts on a buffet table against a stone wall. Light filtered in from high windows. The street noises were hushed here. Rose wanted to find a good place to spend the night. She was eyeing every corner and hall for a forgotten spot the two of them could hide out in for another night. She couldn't afford the high prices of the available lodging.

This hotel was full of banquet rooms and ballrooms, back hallways and courtyards opening onto hidden rooms. Perhaps there was a maid's room or janitors closet tucked in here somewhere. Anna was right, money solved a lot of problems. How can you rely on the kindness of strangers in a place like this? Everyone seemed sad, depressed, consumed by forlorn desperation. Not the place of holy rejoicing she had imagined. The concierge had almost growled at her earlier.

Ah well. They would brave the crowds and visit the Grotto while they were here. She studied the ornate carpet, even that looked inviting. She walked outside to find her sister. She glanced down at the chair she'd left her backpack in. It was gone. Anna must have wandered off with it. She glanced up and down the street and spotted Anna at a shop window. All the shops glowed with light. The streets were crowded. A town that never slept.

"Hey. Do you have my pack?" Rose asked, as she got closer.

"No. Should I?"

Rose ran back to the spot where she had left it and searched all around under the tables and in other chairs. It was gone. Vanished. As if it had never been. No one was around. How long had she been daydreaming in the hotel. She felt a stone drop in her stomach, like a dead weight. She was petrified. She still had her sketchbook but now everything was gone. She put her hand to her neck. The pouch she often carried around her neck with her passport and travelers checks was gone, tucked away into the pack as well. She kept grasping her throat with her fingers as though she could make it reappear there. Gone. Everything; the pouch; checks; passport; clothes; blanket; watercolors; and postcards.

What? God she was lazy. So stupid. What was she thinking? *No backpacks* the sign read on the hotel. She'd dropped it down, and gone in. No one was around. She was longing for a luxury she couldn't afford. What was wrong with her?

Anna followed her to and fro, back and forth. "Your serious? You lost it?" She kept repeating it.

"Of course there is crime in a small town full of so many international strangers. Let's comb the streets and the dumpsters in case someone tossed it," Rose said.

"Wow, I am following your lead because you are my big sister, and now look.I'm still miffed about leaving the yacht."

"What did you think was gonna happen? Bernard was going to sail us to Galveston , Texas?"

"Well, he likes Texas. He could, you know. He could do anything he set his mind to."

"He liked us, didn't he Anna?" Rose voice softened. Just remembering him made her feel better.

"Yes. And you liked him too. Just a bit?"

"Yes."

It was getting later by the minute. The two walked slowly, feeling dejected, towards the Grotto,

From this angle, the slender church spire reached for the sky, and the wings of the church opened up like encircling arms, glowing white in the dusk. The church was pressed at the base of the huge rock wall where the spring had burst forth for Bernadette. It was a sign from Virgin Mary. The white outstretched arms of the church glowed against the darkening sky, and stars came out one by one.

They absolutely *had* to get back to Paris, now. Anna had a few travelers' checks with her. Going to Lourdes had put them 400 kilometers in the wrong direction. Their situation had just gone from poor to broke. All the grubby tourists, and all the plastic rosaries, mixed with the funky sewer smell of illness poisoned Rose's whole experience. They were running out of time. She had to get Anna back to Paris to catch her flight. No matter the exhaustion, they had to go. This was a harsh price to pay for a miracle. Maybe she didn't want one that bad. So many sick people in one place cannot be healthy.

THE ROAD TO PARIS

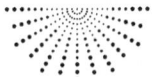

*T*he next morning they were on the road again. Rose faced the prospect of a full day of hitching rides to get to Paris, which was now 800 kilometers away. Her mind fried out trying to put a positive spin on what they had just gone through. Her earlier excitement had melted into pure road weariness. Two very serious girls stood by the side of the ribbon of hi-way that stretched far in both directions. Neither spoke, as what could you say? Rose couldn't blame anyone but herself for her loss.

When you're on the road like this, all you have is each other. She stared at the sun beating a heat wave in to the hard pavement. The sun was enormous and orange as it began its rise. Such a hot color. If she stared at it too long could she go crazy? Like Van Gogh?

There were no cars so far. You don't know that when you hit the road, you just want to be there and be ready. She watched the slow steady un-movement of the sun that just sat on the horizon like a fat Buddha. But it grew smaller as it rose higher. She had never had all day to just stare at the sun. Her face was grim almost frowning. No one wants a frown in his or her car for a long trip. This attitude might not get them any rides. She couldn't control it. She was exhausted. All her hopes had been pinned on the miracle. What did she think? A plastic Mary would arise from the Grotto and find them and touch their foreheads and place kisses on their sun burned cheeks? All the pain and suffering, cries and moans of the sick, and the smells still stuck in her nostrils. She and Anna didn't need help. Not like these forlorn and hopeless did. She should just pray for them all she thought when she saw the snaking line of humanity that crawled past the Grotto of magic healing water. Her own losses were a mere pittance.

Now she stared defiantly at the sun, as the heat shimmered in waves that could be ghosts of all the heroes that ever died in any battle on French soil. How come normal strangers were so nice and helpful and Catholics seemed so selfish? The nuns at the hospital had been quite rude. This trip had made her believe in her ordinary fellowman. Those that helped went beyond. Sharing humor and food as well as rides.

Finally, a car glinted on the distant horizon. She watched without hope, as the speck grew larger. Anna's mood was quiet. They were both standing there half asleep. Finally the car was on them, and then flew past in a whir. The roar as it sped by, was full of promise. Eventually a few cars flew by in the other direction.

"Perhaps we should say a prayer for a safe journey," Rose said.

"Good idea. At this point, a ride would feel like a miracle."

Rose laughed.

Anna smiled.

"God, I have high expectations," Rose sighed.

"I'm gonna sit awhile." Anna dropped unceremoniously to the ground.

"Fine. I'm too mad to sit." Rose knew Anna was upset that they'd left the Riviera and all their new friends. But it had been a valid decision. Anna had a plane to catch. If she missed it Rose would be the one to figure out how to get her home. She couldn't house the two of them in Europe indefinitely. They were in a bad place now; miles from Paris, broke and friendless. Few supplies. Her mind was spiraling in a downward spin. Rose was mad. But she had only herself to blame. "Smile if a car comes." She spoke aloud to herself. She had shrugged off the loss of her backpack and moved on. As she waited the full impact of the loss dawned. She had lost all her travelers checks, her clothes, her passport, and even the warm wool blanket Edith had given her. She had her Frye boots on and her favorite macramé shell necklace. The thought of the loss just made her tired all over again.

ROSE HAD PULLED HER SISTER BACK ON THE ROAD HOME TO be responsible, and spiritual,. Like the miss goody- two shoes she'd been at home: the oldest, and the big success story. She hated to let everyone down now. Yet, she had. She had screwed up royally. They were now in a big disaster. It was all her fault. Now completely broke, and cold besides. She felt like she had a hangover since she was delirious from no sleep and hunger. She didn't even deserve the kindness of strangers if she only resented and judged people. All this frustration, as she watched the pregnant red sun rise higher up, becoming a yellow disc like a shield some Roman guard would wave about in times past. Each car that whizzed by was gone in a whirr of heat wave mirage.

"You know, I am glad we both got to meet Peter," Rose said before they lapsed into silence. She was, but now there was a serious countdown, 'get back to Paris'. An hour later Rose too, sat. "What day is it anyway?"

Anna was sound asleep. All she heard in response was her sister's steady breathing.

A car whizzed by. And Rose didn't even turn her head. This was the kind of day it was. The screeching tires stopped squealing and the car backed up.

Two guys hollered out, "Whoa, where you two babes headed?"

"Paris," Rose said.

"Come wid us. We can get you a ways down de road at least. We're headed to Doferderry Town. Ez great."

"Sure. Great." Without even registering their Spanish accents. Rose helped a still groggy Anna into the car.

When their new ride's drivers spoke with each other in their low guttural Spanish Basque, it was not musical like the Italians, or full of cream like the French. It was low and rough, like skinned knees on pavement. Their voices grated her ears. Rose was glad she was in the back with Anna. She could be sullen and quiet back here while the guys yakked and muttered.

"Hey I'm talking to you leettle lady."

Rose's head jerked up as she kept trying to stay awake and her head fell forward unbidden. She snapped her head up now, wide-awake.

"Why are we turning here?"

"It's a short cut. Safes miles this way."

"OK."

She watched, guarded. Adrenalin kicked in and she was on high alert now. They were talking fast back and forth and laughing. It wasn't a pleasant sound. Rose tapped Anna's arm. She could see she was on alert to.

"Where are you guys from?" Rose asked in a casual tone. Their English was so bad and thick accented she could barely follow.

"*Chtown oph varna. Lay too rist. Cha-cha-cha.*"

She realized that was a form of chuckle.

"Great. *Merci.*"

THE RIDE

*T*he road was curvy, and the men were silent now, driving too fast for narrow winding roads. They blared their horn at the turns to warn oncoming traffic. There wasn't any. Rose swayed side to side in the back seat as they rounded the turns at full speed.

She smiled when she looked at Anna. "Fun ride, hey?" she said in a cherry tone.

Rose was aware that the new silence was ominous. Rose noticed the driver watching Anna in the rearview. Her skin prickled in awareness. She was on full alert. They were in danger. She held Anna's hand undetected in the back seat. They made a silent handshake.

"How long to the next town? Would you mind terribly if I got some sleep back here?"

"*Voulais vous couches sexy babes*? Ve me juest." The driver added.

"Thanks, it's been a long day." She closed her eyes, feigning sleep.

The two guys began speaking rapid fire Spanish in low tones. The guttural noise resembled a growl.

Rose watched out the window, her eyes half slits. She only confirmed that they were in endless miles of nowhere. No houses, no sheep, no towns. She prayed that there would be some farmhouse out here somewhere.

After what seemed miles she spotted some old stone fences. She surmised there must be some sort of homestead out here nearby. She sat up abruptly. "Ooh I'm sick. Soo sick. I'm gonna barf. I hate to do it in your car. Can you pull over?"

The guys looked at each other. Mustache guy told the driver, "*pool ouver.*"

Sure enough, Rose could see a small house just ahead, set back from the road. "Ouhh. I'm gonna be so sick. I can't hold it any more. If you stop I can make it to that ditch over there."

"Wait. *No in me auto,*" the driver barked, and he pulled over and jerked to a stop.

The two girls tumbled out, holding the duffel between them. Mustache took the opportunity to light a cigarette. Rose held her stomach hunched over in pain and lurched over to the ditch. "Anna, can you hold my hair?"

The driver leaned on the car and shook out a cig too. Neither man wanted to witness the disgusting bodily function. Rose kept stumbling groaning moaning. Lurching forward to the top of the ridge.

Anna wailed as she followed, "Rose, what's wrong?"

Rose dropped the duffel and grabbed Anna's hand. She pointed to the stone house on the ridge and took off running. Anna ran too. They headed as fast as they could go, to the house. The men started the car and drove along the road to cut them off. The girls kept running until they reached the back of the house hoping to god someone was home.

A woman in a billowy day dress was out back hanging

laundry on the line. The wind caught a sheet momentarily waving it like a flag. The woman jumped when she saw the two girls. Their faces, white, with hair sticking out all sweaty.

"Please Madame. *Silt-e-plais, Madame.* These men following us, they are *tres mal.*"

The woman left her laundry, wet and sopping, in the straw basket. She shooed them into the farmhouse. She began locking doors. Anna pushed a chair in front of a door.

The men parked in the road and climbed the path to the house. The girls hid in the bedroom, obeying the gestured commands of the woman, who seemed to know exactly how to behave in the face of perceived threat or danger. They watched from the window. Just then the farmer came around from behind the barn holding his pitchfork.

"What do you want- *Ques sue sai,*" he bellowed in French to the men as they panted up the hill towards him.

Rose's heart thudded as she saw the two unshaven men in their black shirts with Elvis collars stuck hard to their sweaty torsos. The mustached one had a thick gold chain bouncing as he ran. The driver was small and sallow skinned. Why hadn't they noticed all this before they got in the car? Rose wondered.

The farmer just stood his ground, all 6 feet and barrel chested. His big arm easily grasped the pitchfork. A few chickens scratched around the yard. A red tailed rooster landed in a tree and began his yodel. The driver stopped dead in his tracks. His face blanched. No sign of the girls anywhere. The rooster flew down from the tree straight at him still yodeling. The second man stopped dead in his tracks and his buddy bumped into him. They both fell into the dust.

"Oh forget eet. *Nefer mine.*" He shouted at the farmer. His yellow skin turning green.

The chickens kept clucking and advancing down the drive. The farmer just stared. His big red beard stuck out making him look like a Norman Viking. Both thugs then turned, and scurried back to their car. Like rats when the lights are turned on. Once the men had gone, the farmer turned, scratched his head and went back to his chores forking hay into the goat pen. The goat bell clanged in the blue air.

| 'Country French Stone Barn"

The farmer's wife went to get the girls. Rose and Anna came out from the back bedroom. She looked at them and shook her head. They both stood frozen and white faced. She shook her head with a stern face and then said cluck - cluck just like a chicken with a twinkle in her eye. At that both girls collapsed into a fit of hysterical laughter. The unexpected relief after their exhaustion and ordeal took them over the edge. The pent up fear and panic dissipated. The image of those slick dark men falling over each other in haste at the site of a few chickens. Shaking with mirth they followed her into the kitchen. She filled a clay pitcher with cool water and with a straight face gestured for them to sit down. She poured them each a glass. And then she too, burst into a jolly belly laugh.

"*Merci*." Rose drained her glass.

Anna sipped her water and looked amused. The woman refilled her glass from the pitcher. Rose glanced around the room with tears in her eyes. "*Merci beaucoup, Madame. Ma s'apelle Rose.* This is *ma seur Anna*."

The plaster walls were painted a cheery yellow-gold. A big oak cupboard filled with pottery took up one wall. The wood kitchen table they sat at was old and solid.

The woman answered in French, "*Je suis Jeanne Marie. Happy to meet you. Those men were tres mal.*" She spun her finger at her head. "*Mal de tete.*"

"*Oui, oui.*" Everyone laughed.

The low ceilinged farmhouse had big wood beams below the plaster. Probably more rooms up there Rose surmised. The large fireplace had an iron pot resting on the hearth. The large kitchen window had a big window seat with gingham pillows on it.

Once she had control of herself, Rose tried to explain. "We were traveling to Paris. We were on the main road, thumbing." Rose gestured with her thumb out. "These guys took a wrong turn and kept winding and winding around through back roads." She gestured with her hands in explanation because her French was so bad.

"We were completely lost," Anna said.

"We have a bag, a duffel, with our things, but we left it out there. Down in a ditch near the side of the road." She gestured out past the fields of sunflowers. "Is this your land?"

"Oh yes, me and Henri have lived here always."

Rose noticed a little rabbit hovered at the edge of the

vegetable garden. The laundry hung dangling crooked on the line.

"Your laundry," Anna said. "Let us help you."

Jeanne Marie gasped, she put her hand to her mouth. She was shocked at herself for forgetting.

"Those guys are long gone," Rose said.

"Vanished." Jeanne Marie snapped her fingers.

The three headed to the yard to finish putting up the white garments, sheets, towels, and overalls that still remained. The farmer called to his wife and came around the corner followed by a couple of chickens. Like an entourage, Rose thought. He nearly jumped out of his skin when he saw the three of them, chatting away in English and a little French.

"Company?" He swiveled his head around searching. "Where did they come from?"

Jeanne Marie just shook her head at him. "Time for *dejeuner.*"

She waved her hand and all traipsed back in to the house. Rose and Anna introduced themselves again and explained about the two men from the city. Jeanne Marie sliced some thick pieces from a fresh loaf of bread that was sitting on a wooden paddle beside the oven. She removed the blue and white cloth from a plate of cheeses and offered it. The farmer displayed a long salami he brought from the larder. Jeanne Marie began to slice the meat, while he went to wash up. He was still shaking his head. He hadn't said anything yet. When he came back chuckling the group gathered around the table.

He passed the salami to Anna. "You try this. This is our specialty."

"Thank you. It looks wonderful."

"Is this goat cheese?" Rose asked.

"Fresh made from our goats."

Rose savored the various cheeses. Unpasteurized and smooth, it tasted so creamy and different than anything she'd tasted before. The group enjoyed lunch and humorous anecdotes about the two Spaniards who'd high tailed it when confronted by this very large farmer.

Anna laughed. "They were afraid of the chickens."

"We left our bag way back there. I hope they didn't grab it. We have to go get it." Rose said.

"Is it valuable?" Jeanne Marie asked.

"It's everything we own." Anna said.

Rose looked down at her plate, oh no, surely they didn't notice that duffel. "I'm sure it's ok," She assured Anna. "We better hurry, just in case." She rose from the table abruptly.

"You stay and rest. I can grab it with the tractor. I'm headed out that way anyway," Henri said. He spoke only French but Rose got the gist.

When Henri returned with a big grin, their duffel and a fresh bunch of wild flowers he'd grabbed. Anna hugged him spontaneously. "For you for the journey."

Henri then drew a map to get them back to the main road. While, Jeanne Marie shrugged at the flowers and packed a lunch with huge slices of bread, cheese, and salami for their travels. Anna arranged the flowers in a jar with water and they perked right up on the kitchen table. Rose added a sprig of the fresh lavender to her hair.

Henri looked up from his elaborate sketch of square fields, streams, and forests, then explained the safest thing for them to do was to cut through the property through various connecting farms and head northwest. This way they could avoid all local roads, and end up near a main hi-way. The back way would emerge on a dirt road that would take them to 371 and the high way to Paris through

Avignon. It was four or five kilometers at most he thought, but definitely the safest way to go.

Rose admired his efforts and would never forget the site of the big red bearded viking like farmer, head bent over the table, sketching. He smiled so big when he explained the way.

INTO THE WOODS

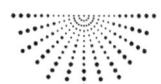

"*I*'m hot. And sticky." Anna complained as they trudged in the August afternoon heat.

"I'll carry the duffel for a while."

"It's all your fault."

"I know," Rose said.

"Aren't you the one who said when you are on the right path the universe helps you?"

"Yes." Rose smiled; she was pleased Anna was getting it.

"We are walking through a field in the dead afternoon heat. Not a road in sight."

"Stating the obvious are we now?"

"Don't patronize me." Anna stopped, put her heavy bag on the grass. "If we had never left the Yacht and Bernard we'd be sailing to Greece by now."

"Perhaps." Rose picked it up and tossed it over her shoulder. She kept on walking.

"Since you made us leave, it has been nothing but disaster. First Lourdes was a mistake—a plague waiting to happen—all that sickness and disease. Then, your backpack, traveler's checks, and passport were stolen. Finally, only a scant two hours of sleep and three solid hours of waiting on the Hi-way with every car zinging by. The only ride we can get, kidnaps us. We must be doing something wrong." She waved her hands at the small white butterflies flitting about. "According to your theory and all."

"Perhaps we are going in the wrong direction?"

"Duh."

"Perhaps we are not in sync with the direction we have chosen?"

Meantime their walk and talk had taken them a long way through the golden wheat fields and moved them into the blessed shade of the forest. The temperature dropped ten degrees in the shade. The sweet scent of honeysuckle filled the woods mixed with pine needles. Lush lime green grass with tiny violet blossoms were scattered on the carpet. Birds were a symphony of sound in the trees. Rose was torn between answering her sister and just inhaling the whole place in. She saw a huge rock, big enough for two. Its mossy blanket looked inviting.

"Time for a rest." Rose swung the duffel down from her shoulder.

She hoisted herself to the top of the rock and leaned back. She stared up at all the trees reaching to frame a cathedral over her head. She didn't want to think, to talk, or to explain. She pulled her skirt up a bit to let the sun warm her bare legs, and just lay there inhaling it all in, tuning in to layers of sound. She tried to distinguish —a hive of bees in the low drone, a chirpy high section; the loud bark of a crow; a coo-coo of the doves. Then suddenly, beneath all of that, she sat straight up.

"I hear water."

They both listened to the distant music of water spilling over rock. It grew louder once they focused on it.

Rose turned to Anna, "Why are we here?"

"Because the farmer told us a short cut to get back to the main road."

Literally that was true. The cross-country route the farmer suggested would give them the means to be on a new Hi-way headed north and they wouldn't cross paths with the Spaniards.

"Why are we here?" Anna's voice squeaked. "What a stupid, stupid question. Where the hell are we in the first place?"

"That's my point," Rose said.

Anna lay there, the peace and solidity of the rock oozing itself into her back. She let go there in the woods. She began to cry.

"Anna? I've never seen you cry. It's OK. Just let it go. Let it all go."

"I try so hard. I try hard to be good and responsible. I work extra hard at the restaurant so my boss will find me indispensable. I saved money to come out here and travel. But traveling is hard too."

"I know."

"And fun." She looked up at Rose through wet eyelashes. "There is so much to decide going back. Whether to go to college—get educated to land a good job. You know?"

"What?"

"It's like we are all on our own all the time regarding the *big LIFE* decisions. There is no one who seems to care. Other people must have grown-ups around who care if you go to college, or make good grades, or flunk out. Find a career... or not."

"Yeah. You put your finger on it. I've been doing that so long I just thought it was normal. Once, in Jr High School, my friend Chelly's father, asked to see my report card. I pulled it out from a book. It was pressed smooth, with this clean row of A's. I was so glad to show it to someone. He said, "Chelly, that's what I'm talking about." Hers had been dirty, folded and stuffed in her back pocket. She smiled and gave mine back. When I replaced it, I realized he was the only adult I had shown it to. I had made all of those A's for me. So I could get into a good High School and then apply to a good college. I wanted to learn as much as I could while in class. And perhaps even go for a scholarship. Or whatever.

"But it's really always true in life. The sooner you start living for yourself—please yourself, please your ideals; your own integrity—the better. Each person *always* has their own agenda in mind. Their own motivations or reasons for acting. It's hard to be young and on our own. I know it's more than that, it's all the other kids too. They're just children. We have to be there for them, if no one else is. Anyway the sooner you grow up, and get on with life, the better. I think Americans tend to be coddled in the nest too long anyway."

"So, do you know where we are?"

"I don't know where exactly, but I do know where we are headed." Rose spoke in a teaching, patient tone. "We are headed to Paris. If we are both sure, and focused on our direction, the trip will unfold more smoothly."

"Families are training grounds really. A safe place to make mistakes in the trial and error of *Life*. I don't know what's up with our parents, but I do know I love them. I value what they have given me and taught me. You are my little sister, but I view you more as an equal. Partly that is how Mom always treated me—like we were running the family and the household together."

"You are the one who asked; why are we here?" Anna said.

"I mean to say, I am glad, so glad to be here in these woods made of peace and blessings—in this strange French wood, right here and now, with you. We were brought here by a series of seemingly disconnected events. But somehow it has brought us closer and deeper together, despite the seemingly random approach."

Anna looked around, her face had brightened, her eyes were open wide. "Maybe so. That scared me to death when we were trapped in the car spinning so fast down the winding roads. I knew they were bad. I had a vibe about it."

"Exactly, I had a vibe, and you had one. So I began praying like crazy for help. Anyway, nothing is random. Things are not always what they seem. No matter someone else's evil intent, everything can be used to bring about good. You have to steer your own ship."

"Ships again. Wish I was on one."

"Pay attention to inner core belief, inner guidance. In life there are always icebergs—unseen, underwater danger, and destruction. We can only be guided if we are listening. Open and willing to listen." Rose stretched her legs and arms and reached for the blue patch of sky. "Why did we head to Lourdes?"

"Easy. For a miracle." Anna smiled; she was ready.

"Yes. And strange as it is, I think the magic is here. Now. In this '*Cathedral of the forest*'. And perhaps Bernadette knew that. As a fourteen-year-old girl, who loved the birds, and streams, and woods, she carried that life in her soul. Then Mother Mary appeared to her in the Grotto. Mother Mary chose her. Perhaps Bernadette resonates with you, as a fellow teen seeker. And wanted us to come here—to the deep middle-of-nowhere church in Nature. Where God can be felt, and heard, and miracles can happen."

"Bernadette died in 1879," Anna said.

"The spirit never dies. And love never dies," Rose said. "Two things that are eternal. I am beginning to feel a ton better. And lots of energy."

"Me too, and I cannot understand it."

"You don't have to. Perhaps God and miracles are right here in these Narnian woods."

WITH A NEW LILT AND BUOYANT STEP, ROSE BOUNCED OFF the rock and stretched. "Let's find that water."

They went down to a small grotto, where water was running icy, a miniature waterfall into a small pool. Each of the girls drank handfuls of the spring water and splashed their arms and legs. This water was sweet and clear. Watercress and mint grew in bunches amidst the rock mossy ledges. When they were sated, Rose picked up the duffel and Anna helped her adjust it on her back.

They tiptoed through the spongy loam soil that formed a path through the woods. They were headed North so the sun was on their left. Rose savored each step in these woods, enveloped by a feeling of peace. She was a little wary of the highway now. But if she were to trust her own advice, she knew better.

"I am looking forward to getting back to Paris," Anna stated. "I like the idea of having a few days to explore the city before my return flight. It would be great if we could stay on our own there too, and not go back to our Aunts apartment until the last day." Anna realized she loved hanging out with her sister. They made a great duo.

"You want to hang with me?" Rose heart gave a sweet twinge, at the gesture of forgiveness in her sister's tone.

"That is my wish."

Rose felt like hugging Anna. After all her mistakes and flaws as a big sister, Anna was ready to try again. She felt forgiven. In what seemed like no time at all, their buoyant strides brought them to the edge. And there before them was a paved road, the hi-way smooth and straight —a road to somewhere.

"To Paris!" Rose cheered.

2 8

FATHER AND SON

*B*ack on the hi-way, still glowing from there sacred time in the woods, the girls felt pure glee. They danced around the empty road. The very next car that came their way, stopped. The driver, with wavy sandy hair, wire frame glasses, and a big smile, spoke French so articulately, Rose could understand him.

"*Bonjour. Ca Va? Mon fils et moi* are going to Avignon for a convention. Can we offer you a lift?"

"Thank you kindly. I am Rose and this is my sister Anna. We are on our way to Paris. I believe that will get us half way there."

"*Bonne! Ascende la.* Get in."

Jacques and his son Tomas told them all about their plans. "We are scientists. We are headed to a Tesla Convention. Have you ever been to Avignon?"

"Never have."

"It's a great medieval city. You girls will enjoy visiting it."

Anna and Rose relaxed. They could enjoy the enthu-siasm these two had about their trip. They talked with fervor about the convention. Many scientists planned to attend. They would bring their latest inventions and share new discoveries about free energy.

Dusk approached as they drove into Avignon. The medieval city seemed forbidding with high stone walls and cobblestone streets. As darkness encroached, and the city shut down for the night, Rose was glad they would have the day to explore it tomorrow. Jacques and Tomas insisted the girls share a nice meal and a nights rest before continuing their journey. Jacques had offered to phone Aunt Edith and let her know they were safe and in good hands. Rose blanched at that.

When they entered the hotel lobby, Rose and Anna excused themselves to go freshen up and use the ladies room. Jacques purchased a newspaper. While they waited in the lobby, with a sherry before dinner, Jacques and Tomas spoke rapidly in French, clearly excited. When the girls returned, Jacques offered them each an aperitif. Rose and Anna sipped appreciatively. They took in the new surroundings, while the men continued conversing at a speed that did not include Rose. She knew they both felt at ease here as the crowded lobby filled with crinkled linen suits and worn leather briefcases. Anna lifted her amber liquid to Rose. They didn't have to speak to get it. There was an excited buzz as the large lobby full of comfy couches filled up with mostly men scattered in small groups casually leaning on sofas in wrinkled shirts and worn shoes. Papers spilled on coffee tables with excited voices sharing ideas, or emphatic, expressive discourse, as more colleagues arrived for the weekend convention.

WHEN SHE GOT UP FROM THE COMFORTABLE SOFA IN THE lobby, to follow the party to their table, Rose glanced at the tossed newspaper left open to an inside page on the coffee table. There was a photo of the gambler that had visited Riviera Bernard on what had been their last night on the yacht. Tilting her head sideways, she could just make out the headline:

PLAYBOY INTERNATIONAL

Jacques and Tomas spoke mainly to each other. It was clear Jacques wanted Tomas to feel comfortable at his first convention. There were a few women here as well. But they blended right in, dressed in brown tweed shirt-dresses or skirts with spectacles and untidy buns, bulging briefcases and eager enthusiasm from bright sparkling eyes. Not knowing the language was a problem, Rose knew, but as she found herself listening, the excitement and thrill in the tones and voices was a kind of music—a vibration like a triumphal symphony. She feared it was all way above her head—in whatever language.

The idea of dinner was an honor and a welcome treat. They had been well fed at the farmer's house. Yet still she anticipated a good meal.

The Music played subtly in the background. It was familiar Edith Piaffe tunes. And a French version of *My Way*. As the crowd grew it drowned it out for the most part.

While at diner with the father that was younger than their father, and the son that seemed young and eager as a younger brother—although he was about 16—they had amazing discussions. Rose and Anna enjoyed the dinner, a long one, wine paired with each course. Rose wisely refrained from the French habit, and instead she drank slow enough so she could forgo each new offer of a pour. The jovial talk about the Science convention resumed. Rose appreciated the contrast of sitting in a stone courtyard surrounded by medieval and Roman structures, while listening to stories about Nicola Tesla and free energy. Clearly the French did not live in the past.

Jacques, ever the gentleman, had already insisted on getting the girls a room together. It was necessary so they could shower and get cleaned up.

They discussed the latest scientific discoveries, which was the main reason for their attendance at the New Science Conference held annually in France. This year it was Avignon. The Noetic Sciences were a worldwide institute that celebrated the most cutting edge proven or unproven discoveries. The idea was to spark the imagination of the possible. So much had begun with Nicola Tesla who never had enough time to follow through with all of his ideas. The ones he managed to develop were only the tip of the iceberg of knowledge and human potential locked in his imagination.

Jacques, Mr. Geno, yet he preferred the first name basis with these young Americans, pushed his thick unruly locks behind his ears.

"Tell me, do you two know much about Nicola Tesla?" His head swiveled back and forth to look them each in the eye. "Eeh? Well now, Tesla slaved on his inventions. Not to invent them, but he worked to build them and prove to doubters what was possible with electricity.

"As work at this scale was extremely expensive, his time went to raise money and awareness of the possible, and attract investors. He longed to experiment with the machine once he made it. He knew we could have free energy. While he had millions of ideas, and he patented many of them, he had so much more to do. The inventions burst forth in his brain fully formed. When he explained his ideas, he sounded pompous and narcissistic explaining them as fact. Ideas and concepts others had never conjectured, or even imagined were possible. He worked hardest trying to get the big players to be aware of all the magnificence that could be accomplished. He could envision a free-electricity world, which would free mankind on many levels.

"Much of what has become normal, in the tech revolution, was made possible by his inventions from the early 1900's. Although he lived a long life, no one could understand his peaceful purpose with machines."

Rose was spell bound. "He must have been so lonely. You know, with no one who could understand him."

There was a moment of silence as those at the table took it in.

"Yes indeed," Jacques continued. "That is why we now dedicate this new research convention to him. We are here to listen to one another's crazy theories; or to build some of Tesla's inventions. The world at that time decided to use Einstein's theory of relativity to aid in the creation of an atom bomb; a destructive force, rather than a creative one. Tesla's theory of relativity, in 1890, was $E = M V2$, Using ether for air. V-Velocity. He knew the speed of light was not the fastest speed in our universe."

"He never married because he was devoted, passionate about his chosen vocation. The messages –blue prints in his mind were like fully formed downloads. He had to draw the diagrams and build the inventions. His efforts turned to dust before his eyes. He watched as his scientific experiment station was destroyed. The world was not helpful, or grateful, or supportive."

"My dad is an inventor and an engineer. He put that curiosity and belief system into our gene pool," Anna said.

"I love to problem-solve. And download new concepts. That is what I love about architecture," Rose said.

"You know, Tesla got connected right away. He knew

everyone; Edison, Westinghouse, JP Morgan. But it didn't help his plight. Somehow it worked against him."

"Perhaps they were jealous, envious of his genius," Anna said.

"He knew electricity should be free because it could travel using the earth as a medium, with out wires. No wires were necessary. Therefore; little expense in building it, or maintaining it. He invented the telegraph. He even suggested the electric car,- because then transportation would be free."

"All the financiers you mentioned made a living by charging a lot for all of those things. Especially energy," Anna said. She knew a lot about financiers.

"Exactly, jealous, greedy men used their influence and wealth to discredit him, ruin his reputation, and destroy what he built. He died in 1943 at age 86, an unknown hero. All of us at the convention get together to honor him and explore Tesla's ideas further."

WHEN MR. GENO FINISHED, SPARKS FLEW FROM HIS EYES. He himself was a biologist. He had been following the work of Dr. Bruce Lipton, who had coined the term epigenetics only recently. This was life changing in the field of health and wellness. Rose and Anna shared that they had been raised to distrust doctors and medicine—like pharmaceuticals—on principle.

Anna volunteered, " *'we are only as young as the spine is supple.'* To quote my great grandmother."

"I can explain the scientific truth of that statement," Jacque said. "But first, how has that maxim affected you so far in your life?"

Rose piped in, "That's a quote from our great Gramma Amelia. She raised my Mom with all sorts of old world sayings. She came over on a boat from Europe when she was 17, but we don't know what country she was from, or her nationality for that matter."

"I think she was a gypsy," Anna interrupted.

"Yes, she was wise, and seemed to have some psychic powers, so we romanticized her into some sort of a Gypsy," Rose said. "Well, both my Mom, and our Uncle are real health and exercise fanatics. When we were young, my mom enrolled all of us in gymnastics. I spent my youth doing back bends, walkovers, and cartwheels. My sister Murielle is a star gymnast. She had all the younger ones tumbling and cartwheeling and doing aerials in the front yard. My mom still goes to the gym to work out three times a week. Our uncle was in the Marines and he is now a mid-weight boxer. He is trim and youthful. Our grand-mother walks miles daily."

"Yes," Jaques mustache twitched at the long answer his question had inspired. " It has affected generations of your family, I see." He cleared his throat. "We were born to move, and use our bodies. The spine is a key secret." Jacques said. "Even going way back to the ancient Egyp-tians. The pharaohs held that the spine is sacred. That is why in Egyptian art the spine is always concealed. You see the front of the body and the face and feet in profile. Let me explain. Have you ever heard of chakras"?

"Sure I have," Rose said.

Anna looked bored.

"But that has to do with Indian or Hindu spirituality, not science," Rose added.

Tomas smiled. He knew what was coming. He knew about all of it.

"I have friends that sit around meditating," Rose said. "They discuss chakras and astral projection and stuff. They are pale and stoned. I do not think of them as scientifically advanced." Rose looked doubtful. "There are groups of new-agers who share houses and live communally in Montrose and Austin."

"Hippies." Anna said the word with disdain. She was way to Cosmo for that.

Jacques nodded. He pushed back from the table and assumed a relaxed posture. He patted his breast pocket for his pipe, and glanced around for a light. He pulled out his pipe and placed it on the ashtray. The gesture reminded the girls of their dad, he smoked a pipe. Jacque glanced around the ornate restaurant. Dark paneled and low light in crystal chandeliers and wall sconces. White tablecloths glowed under silver candlesticks.

"This world is far away from your hippie friends."

"Acquaintances," Rose corrected. "Yes, you seem normal like my family in Paris. Those hippie guys are fringe."

"Yes, well scientists and technology are part of the advanced mainstream culture. Chakra is a Sanskrit word."

"Wait. What about Egypt?"

"Yes. Ancient cultures have a lot in common with each other. More so than with our modern culture. Chakra is a term common in India." He waved the waiter over. "Desert anyone?" He glanced around at eager faces. "Can you bring us a display tray of the house specialties?"

At dinner, Anna was having so much fun she had forgotten her diet and cleaned her plate. She ate asparagus with hollandaise and braised lamb chops. Well that's on her diet, Rose realized. The waiter returned with a large silver tray, on which was displayed a variety of tarts, choco-late mousse, and crème brûlée.

Rose was on the edge of her seat. Two worlds that she thought were far apart, middle-class scientists and fringe hippie-dom, were about to collide. Her brain that kept things well separated, as if her life were made of separate stories she was reading, was being breached. She usually loved chocolate mousse, however, today she was in the mood for apple tart.

"Rose will have the mousse," Anna spoke up, "it has no bread. I will have the crème brûlée.

Jacques directed the waiter to bring their deserts and coffees to the lounge. He was ready for his pipe.

On the trip back through the lobby, Rose took in the scene. The excited crowd buzzed; as the large lobby full of comfy couches and chairs was now, completely packed. Grown scholars, young and old, sat on sofa arms and scattered jackets and briefcases and papers on every available surface. Neither Anna nor Rose spoke as they took in the thrill of energy around them.

SCIENCE MEETS THE SPIRITUAL

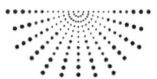

Once they were settled, in the leather couch and armchairs, the waiter offered Jacques a light. He lit his pipe and puffed to get it going.

"Chakras are to the guru's in India, spiritual centers in the body. There are seven of them, in a line down the spine. They have names, are assigned spiritual colors, and have a spiritual function as well. Yet, to a scientist, a biologist, they are each associated with a physical gland in the body. These glands are regulated by the endocrine system, which is a part of the autonomous nervous system. Do you know what that is?"

"No," Anna said. "Good brûlée."

"Does it run on its own? Without conscious help?" Rose asked. "In a healthy body?"

"There are seven glands, 1st, the root chakra at -the tip of the spinal column are the gonads, whose color is red."

Before he could say another word, Tomas chimed in, "Second:Sacral/Leydig cells–orange, third: the Solar plexus/adrenals -yellow; fourth: heart/thymus -green, fifth: throat/thyroid-Blue, sixth: third- eye/pineal gland-indigo, and the seventh chakra is the crown/pituitary gland-violet." Tomas eager, named them all quickly.

Rose shook her head. It was too much to memorize, but they had made their point. "I know in the Indian-guru version, each is tied to the 4 elements as well."

"Each of the seven centers run in a straight line up the spine. At the base of the spine one can activate the whole system with the kundalini energy."

"Yes," Rose said, "I've heard of that, too. It's always depicted like a dragon or something. Wow, this seems like myths. I listen to these stories as though they are concepts; abstract. Like the myths we have about Roman and Greek gods; old stories that have become a part of our Western culture. I had assumed these concepts were the Eastern version. Now, you are saying it's all true. Stories to illustrate real scientific facts about the body."

"As healthy as you are, you probably feel the kundalini energy too, at times. You just have to become aware. It's like a tingling at the base of the spine. It functions like an energy battery that zings through the body—through all the aligned chakras. And then it activates the pineal and pituitary glands in the head."

"So interesting, the seven chakras refer to real glands, meaning the physical part of us is deeply tied to the spiritual," Rose interjected.

"Back to my initial point, exercise is crucial. Certain kinds of exercise anyway, keeps you flexible. Flexible spines keep the Chakras open and spinning. You know, like yoga practice, which focuses on flexibility. And also like gymnastics, as your family is in the habit of doing. Do you meditate?"

"No," Rose said. "I do pray though, I pray all the time."

"Well, when you do—meditate or pray--and you practice stillness, you can become conscious of all of these chakras, glowing and spinning. You can concentrate and move energy from the earth, through each one. If you go slowly, you can become aware of each one pulsing inside you, regulating health. Thus the spiritual centers are linked to the physical glands that regulate hormones in the healthy body. When everything is aligned and working, if injured, you heal quickly. The body is a miracle, a living daily miracle."

Rose and Anna had troubled looks. "We are seeking a miracle," Rose explained. "We just came from Lourdes. There are so many sick people there."

Anna wrinkled her nose. "I have never seen so many sick people, so much disease."

"Yes, many diseases happen when the system fails. Stress is one of the biggest factors in system failure. Stress usually stems from fear. Fear, lack, worry, paranoia--totally suppresses the immune system. How do you suppose it does that?"

"It's not positive?" Anna offered.

"Not joyful or hopeful," Rose added.

"Fear constricts and blocks blood flow. And therefore constrains the spinning and pulsing of the chakra/glands. The immune system is the army for the body. It wages a constant war of protection against the enemy of foreign contagion on the host body."

"Like white sugar. We were told not to touch the stuff because it was white poison. Too refined and stripped of anything of value for the body. We were told to avoid it like the plague. We only had sweets on Sundays. We had a diet of green vegetables and broth to keep us healthy," Rose said. "There are nine of us."

"Our parents didn't have health insurance," Anna explained.

"Well, your parents are wise. Health is the real insurance."

"Yes, I know that feeling. I feel naturally high," Rose said. "That's why I never do drugs."

There was a low fire burning in the stone fireplace. By now Jacque was quite relaxed, settling back in the deep leather chair by the hearth. The smell of wood smoke mingled with the smells of tobacco. At some point he'd signaled for a brandy and was sipping it. The smells of brandy and aromatic tobacco brought memories of their Dad to Rose and Anna. A comfortable silence enveloped them, as each settled into his own reverie. It was late now, nearly midnight.

In her mind, Rose pictured the diagram of the cross-legged Buddha figure with the seven chakras' lined up in a row of colored discs. She had always thought of the spiritual world as more conceptual and invisible. Not physical at all. Like she sensed angels were *real* benevolent beings, even though they were invisible. Weren't they? Her dad had said sometimes angelic help was sent in the form of a dog or another animal. She wished her dad were here to meet Jacque. Jacque would fit right in with him and his friends. Her dad's friends had solstice celebrations around big fires in the woods. They were mostly women dressed in colorful kaftans and doted on him, calling him an old soul. He was old all right, Rose thought. He clapped his hands over his head and danced around the fire like a Greek sailor, or Zorba, with his long black hair and dark beard streaked with silver. When his balalaika friends played their drums and instruments, and he began to dance, everyone thought he looked like Zorba the Greek.

Rose thought of her family. Her Uncle was a priest and a scientist. He was so proper and middle class—correct and above reproach. Her dad on the other hand, was a new age free spirit—photographer- artist, who smoked a pipe, and carried on going to parties with all his European friends. He wasn't a hippie, but he had a beard— he was really a free spirit. Their mom, who loved to sing, had long thick black hair, with bangs that made her look like Joan Baez. They were into folk music, not rock and roll. They had been had so good together. No wonder Anna was convinced.

How could all this new info on chakras and self-healing help heal a *family*?

Jacques broke her reverie, "I know I just launched into a lot of detail here, I was trying to illustrate that science and spirituality are very closely related. Spiritual beliefs that have been part of ancient cultures forever, mostly Eastern spiritual beliefs that we don't really embrace in the conservative West, are actually being proved to be true through the scientific experiments in the West."

"East meets West," Rose nodded.

"The main point is, the old model of Newtonian physics is no longer true. Ancient beliefs—that we generally ignore like a bunch of mumbo-jumbo—are actually closer to the truth."

"Wow, it almost seems like a conspiracy," Anna said.

"How so?" Jacques asked.

"The medical establishment keeps us in the dark. We, in our family, were always taught to view doctors as the enemy." Anna said.

"Great Gramma Amelia had told Mom not to trust doctors, or drugs, or medicine," Rose said. "She gave Mom natural remedies like apple cider vinegar and honey, and lots of vitamin B. We were only allowed whole grain bread as it is filled with b vitamins, never white bread. All the beneficial nutrition is stripped out when they process white flour.

"Our Mom had observed that smoking was prevalent at the same time white bread hit the market en mass and invaded the country. Once the valuable niacin was removed from the wheat, people were no longer getting enough B vitamins. The body then craved the nicotine found in tobacco to calm excessive nervousness. A natural craving turned into a tobacco addiction. We end up with an anxiety-ridden society that smokes to calm down. Smokers with a serious habit crave cigarettes as if it were oxygen. Smoking calms nerves, just like the B vitamins, niacin, thiamin, and B12 do, which occur naturally in whole wheat bread.

"Mom's into holistic medicine," Anna explained. "We are supposed to get what we need from the food we eat. Not manufactured drugs or pills."

Jacques nodded his head in agreement. "Your mom sounds wise. What you say makes a lot of sense. We French love good food. We stick to the old ways as they have been working for centuries."

Tomas eyes were bright with health. "May I have a brandy father?"

"Not tonight son, some other time."

Of course, they had all enjoyed a nice glass of Bordeaux with their meal. It was the French custom to take wine with meals. In contrast to many American teens, who were raised on sodas.

At Tomas disappointed look, Jacques changed his mind. "How about if you all share one?"

"That's the spirit. It feels like a holiday," Rose said. "By the way, who are the speakers at the conference?"

"They're scientists and PHD's from all over; Europe, India, China, and England."

"So, if they agree that we can heal ourselves, that's

awesome news." She waited a beat. "And yet, there are so many sick people at Lourdes, waiting for a miracle."

"Once serious diseases take such a hold on the body's system, it becomes difficult to heal," Jacques said. "Once the body is so far gone you need drastic measures. You have to heal the mind first, the belief system, before you can heal the body."

"Perhaps that is why miracles work? Devout people really believe in Mary," Rose said. "And in Healing."

"Bad habits can begin as early as a babe in the womb of the mother. Then continue in the homes of those who don't know any better. Then a baby, that began innately normal and healthy, through a poor environment, can spiral downhill. The systems that are in place to create a healthy ecosystem of life, become compromised through the environment, and then it's difficult to regain a healthy balance. And yet," he leaned in conspiratorially, "once someone changes their life and habits,"

"And mind," Rose interrupted, riveted.

Jacques nodded and continued, "The whole system that was spiraling down, can simply reverse everything, and support the body in a healthy direction. You see, the body keeps making new fresh cells. The only thing holding us back is knowledge."

"Aha," Rose said. "It's a commandment after all. 'Know Thyself.' "

"Self-knowledge means more than we thought it did. It was the Greeks who said that, Plato. He is not in the bible." Jacques pointed out.

"Ok," Rose conceded. "But not before God. Or Truth."

"To the Greeks, God was truth," Jacques reminded her.

"Do you think they had all of this figured out?"

"Hard to know. There were so many books burned in the burning of the library in Alexandria."

"And again in the middle ages."

"Conspiracy. I told you." Anna nodded like a wise sage.

"On that note, we have a big day tomorrow. Perhaps we should call it a night."

"Why not, it's only midnight." Rose looked over and noticed that Anna and Tomas had begun a Chess game and were both concentrating.

At this lull in the discourse, Rose suddenly realized she had completely forgotten about the Riviera gambler. She wondered how to find out more. She realized they had been spared meeting him. He had been whisked below deck quite swiftly. The room had become choked with cigar smoke, she could smell it in the corridor. As it was to be their last night, she'd been glad for an excuse to hang in the fresh sea air.

Rose twirled her glass of desert wine, barely sipping, as she pondered all that had been said.

Jacques and she watched the two, as they seemed completely absorbed in the game.

Tomas captured Anna's queen with his knight. The game would be down hill from there.

"Will you be our guests in attending the conference?" Jacques asked. "Dr. Bruce Lipton will be there."

"Oh, I would love to." Rose meant it. "Anna has a round-trip ticket back to Texas. I am trying to get her back to Paris so she doesn't miss it. High school starts at the end of August, and all of that." Her voice sounded wistful to her own ears. "Thank you for the invitation, and dinner, and" she opened her hands encompassing the room, "Everything."

Tomas said, "Check mate."

Anna shrugged.

"Good game," he said jovially and smiled.

"Tomas is the captain of the chess club at school, looks like you had him on the run there for a bit."

"Our Dad loves chess, he never teaches us anything about it though," Anna said.

"Well, your instincts are good. You are a bit of an aggressive player."

"OK," Anna smiled at the unexpected compliment. "Off we go."

"Enjoy a good nights sleep and we will see you at breakfast."

"Thank you so much for our room. It is truly splendid."

"Thank you both for the charming company," Jacque said.

"A tout de l'air," Rose called.

"Bonne hui," Anna mumbled.

"Good night," Tomas said, in such a cute accent.

NIGHT VISIONS

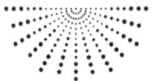

*L*ater that night, as Rose lay in white down comforters and stared at a high white ceiling, classical music played softly in the distance. She thought about her life. She'd sort of jumped out of hers and gone on vacation so she could make some big decisions; decisions about herself and her Life as a free, over-eighteen, single adult. She spread eagle on the bed, listening to Anna snoring lightly in the next one. She reminisced at how Anna could swiftly see how intention worked. They wanted Lourdes—a ride appeared. Now headed to Paris–a ride so fast and wonderful…and safe. Frankly it was spooky. You could test it best on the road. Actually, bad rides reflected a bad attitude quickly, as well. You could think the happy thoughts—change your attitude, change your life. Traveling meant a life *on the road*. She wouldn't be able to live that way forever. Ah, her gypsy soul would perhaps, one day, have to settle down. Perhaps. Perhaps…

Rose was glad Mr. Geno had invited Anna and her to join them. She realized it had been for his son. He probably wanted to ensure there were some young people in the mix. The convention was comprised of mostly older scientists, a few college coeds, and few if any teens.

Rose thought *life* is what made her the sum total of who she is today, right now this minute. Anna and she had prayed for the miracle of her parents return to sanity for everyone's sakes. But God's in charge of this drama we call life. A miracle will occur. Perhaps not the one we are expecting. Would it be them accepting their lives now as it is? Taking it as it comes? Accepting things was after all a valid concept. If you know who you are; you can build from there.

Meaning: Rose could accept her responsibilities and move back home to help her siblings now that she knew what disasters were lurking. On the other hand, she had survived by leaving—by being self-reliant and not expecting anything. She shared all her earnings and only kept enough to survive at a subsistence level. Consequently, she was extremely grateful for whatever opportunity came her way. Attitude was part of that. She labored away, working hard, but was perpetually into self-denial.

Ignorance had been good too. She'd gone off, neither asking, nor expecting help. She contributed her savings freely in the summer. She kept only enough to survive. She was a survivor. On this trip she was becoming far more educated about art and architecture than she could warming a seat at University. It had been the first three years there that had opened her eyes to what she was seeing. So the two went hand in hand. All this knowledge, would surly fuel her career. When she made something of herself, she would help out again; in a more substantial way.

Rose pondered their new situation. What a day. It was an amazing story. It took her mind off of the wild disaster at the beginning of their day. She certainly hadn't wanted to bore their new friends with the details of their chaotic adventure. These new concepts were something she and Anna could use to transform their lives now. Living in the moment meant embracing the present, not dwelling on the past. Her parents' divorce was part of the past.

If there is a microcosm in the macrocosm of the body, then their individual lives are the microcosm in the macrocosm of their family. And the family is the microcosm in the macrocosm of society as a whole. If there is something wrong in the microcosm, it affects the whole—and so on and so on. The family was that important. The tear in the fabric of their particular family unit, the divorce, was playing havoc with the rest of the body of the family. If she could make an analogy with the healing system Jacque had been discussing, there was a definite clue here. A family should be able to fight disease, similar to the way the body does. There were hidden enemies everywhere. Also happiness. That was the true barometer of success. Was it really Plato who had said, *'know thyself'*? Why had she thought it was a commandment? That proclamation was *that* important to her. She could *love* herself, if she *knew* herself. Love has a lot to do with everything. Loving the body surely set up healing vibrations inside of it. Oh yeah, vibes were a hippie thing not a science thing. And yet Jacque had said, the two concepts are only separate in a dualistic universe, therefor not the *Truth*. In Ancient cultures, science and spirituality were very much connected. The whole term witch doctor, the sacred priest, was the healer or doctor. Demons and disease were always thought to be connected in the psyche in indigenous cultures.

If self-knowledge is key, I must know myself not as separate from the whole, but as connected. This is not a commandment from one of Moses' tablets on the mountain, but from science. Scientists are such a big part of our evolution as a species. Those in the *know*, don't use drugs, because they know we don't need them. Cocaine is a white substance that began as a flower. It falls into the same no-no as white sugar and white bread. Refined to the point of being a chemical. If I ate the entire flower, my life might be different. My trip or experience might be quite different. How many flowers does it take to make the white powder? How much do you need to get high? Her thoughts circled round, going back to her family. All of whom she loved dearly. Her mind racing, her body in complete comfort, no longer felt fatigued.

Anna was right. That is why they needed a miracle. A miracle is something you cannot do on your own without God, or Divine Intervention. They had grown up praying for miracles. Every time the car wouldn't start, they prayed for one. Then they would hit that green sedan on the hood just so, and it would start.

In the morning, Rose washed her face in the clean white hotel bathroom. She studied her green eyes in the mirror. Whatever I need to do, I will do. She told herself. I will survive. I have the brains and the will to survive and become someone. I know I am not alone, but all the help around me seems to be invisible—except these new friends. This comfy bed was real indeed.

What do they really want anyway? When you are giving, when is it enough? She needed sleep. She closed her eyes, and finally, sleep was like a coma.

§❧

THE NEXT MORNING WHEN THEY MET JACQUE FOR breakfast, they found him engrossed in the paper. The headline read:

"PLAYBOY INTERNATIONAL' 'Le joueur de
renom, Mr. George Fourlis, a été vu pour la
dernière fois sur le yacht Princessa.

Rose could just make out something like, *Renowned
gambler was last seen on the yacht.* And the name, *Yvette Alexi.*
That was the opening Rose needed. She had no idea how
to begin. She launched in."Jacque what is that on the
headline? Gamblers? It reads like fiction." Rose seemed to
be teasing, or sarcastic. She had not a care in the world
about a European gambler, or a Yacht.

"Hmm?" Jacque was startled. He was engrossed in a
long article deep in the paper. What's that?

"Oh, I noticed the headline of the paper you're reading, something about gambling. Is that at the Riviera?"

"It's just about how you say in America, millionaire?
Mr. Fourlis, his father's mega rich, he's always getting some
publicity about his extravagances. I'm not sure what it is
about this time." He accommodatingly stopped his reading
and folded the paper so he could examine the story.

"PLAYBOY INTERNATIONAL' 'Le joueur de
renom, Mr. George Fourlis, a été vu pour la
dernière fois sur le yacht Princessa, propriété de la
Comtesse Russe, Yvette Alexi.'.

Rose sat beside him on the sofa so she could see more
clearly. "So who is he?"

Rose mind flashed back to her first long talk with
Bernard. He'd approached Anna, a young teen girl, and a

grown man. Soon they were all three animated and headed to his place—which turned out to be a yacht. He had been lonely, she felt it. Loneliness isn't a crime. He was genuinely friendly. She could read people—they both could. He was fine. It seemed he loved hanging with them and needed a friend, despite his friends.

Jacques was saying. "He is a renowned gambler and his game is poker. The rich are masters at throwing money away. But poker is a game of skill. He, I think, is more ruthless than skillful."

Rose thoughts were consumed with Bernard. "So no big deal?" She nodded, "Merci. It's just the picture caught my attention."

Jaques, smiled amused, "*Il est tres normale* with those at the Riviera, we do not take notice anymore." Rose felt sheepish. She kept to her own thoughts as Jaques returned to his paper.

Then when Bernard told her he wasn't the son of a millionaire but a self-made man, she'd thrilled at that detail. Entitled is such an attitude. Creating something with ones wits is another matter. A businessman who had seized the opportunities life gave him and ran with it. He had clearly run all the way to the top, where his life was now a mixture of travel and luxury, along with a type of business. She was naïve and accepting. In the back of her mind she wanted to believe he was good and honest and trust worthy. It's true the boat had remained moored for several weeks with no plans for departure. Then quite abruptly, on the final night everything had changed. Boom. Suddenly the ship was ready to sail. She had the feeling he had been waiting for something.

In her fantasy life she could see herself with Bernard. She wanted to do the right thing by Anna and see her safely on her plane back home. But in truth she had become quite enamored of Bernard.

"I know what you're thinking," Anna intruded on her reverie. You may not realize it, but you were a bit rude to Bernard and he was nothing but a gentleman."

"I know. It's weird. Gerard was so fun to dance with. I didn't know I was being rude."

"Bernard was our host, so it's common courtesy and all that."

Rose mentally kicked herself. She played hard to get beyond the point, and into rudeness, which wasn't desirable. It was unforgivable. She turned red at the thought. She had clearly blown what ever opportunity there may have been.

Wow, she had made a mess of things. Now she'd lost her backpack, and passport, and all of her money. She was the older sister—the responsible one.

Her mind held the fantasy of meeting up with Bernard in Florence perhaps. Yes later on in the fall. He'd hinted more than once that he had a place in Florence. It was on the piazza across the street from the Uffizzi Palace. The sculpture of Michelangelo's David was there. She planned to make a trip to see that at any rate. She chided herself for those past fantasies.

She recalled that once the gambler,—she guessed he was Mr. Fourliss—had shown up, everything had become all hush-hush and exclusive. Bernard transformed into a hard edged and steely eyed businessman. On the surface he was cool and professional. But in the glint in his eye she could see barely concealed revulsion. It was clear he detested this new visitor.

"Ruthless as in criminal interests or malicious intent?" Rose asked, voicing her thoughts. Thankfully Bernard had intercepted him and sent him below deck in a very hushed manner. Neither Rose nor Anna had crossed paths with the newcomer.

"Well, when the rich are involved in gambling, there is a lot of money, or even property at stake. I do not run in those circles, but in my gut I do not like him much."

One thing she did catch and that was his name. Mr. Fourliss was Greek, and he had boarded the yacht and now the Princessa was in the papers. What was going on? Was it gambling or something else? She racked her brain. She was trying to remember a forgotten detail of conversation. She had been focused on getting Anna back to Paris and the timing was perfect. When she had tried to leave before, everyone stopped them. Once the gambler arrived, everyone seemed eager for them to be gone.

It was almost rude, yet it had been the opening she needed. Perhaps the universe was protecting Anna and her from something. She tuned back in to Jacques.

"Like I said, poker is a game of skill and mathematical probabilities. It's actually a fascinating subject. Did you know that it is more likely when tossing a coin to have 6 tails in a row, than to go back and forth consecutively?"

"Amazing." Rose's mind was too distracted to discuss mathematical theories of probability. She just didn't know what questions to ask about Mr. Fourliss or Bernard or the yacht Princessa. She didn't want to explain her encounter there. Perhaps she could find an American paper and have a more detailed understanding. But wait, Bernard was Italian, yet he was with a Russian countess and a Greek tycoon had boarded the boat. How are these things connected?

Jacques looked up closing the paper.

"Good morning Anna!" How was your sleep? Another beautiful day."

His enthusiasm was contagious. Rose decided to let it drop. You know, 'be her now', she was and she could.

PARIS

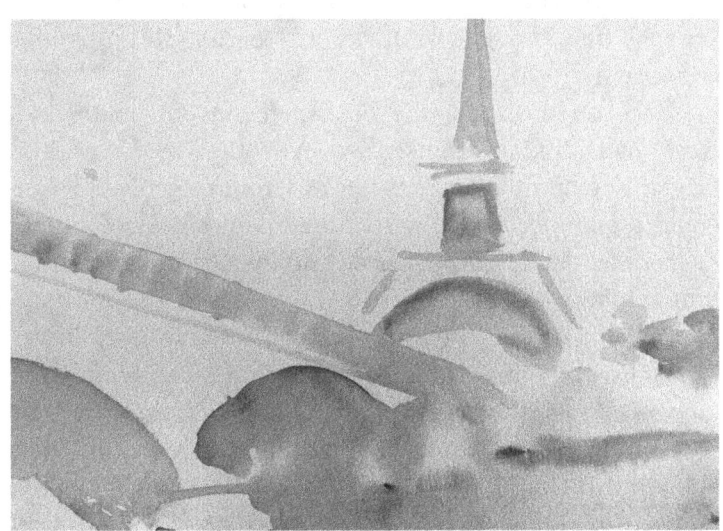

PARIS

| 'The Eiffel Tower'

31

TED

$\mathcal{B}$ack on the road, this time with a renewed sense of well-being, Anna and Rose were ebullient. The rest of the trip was uneventful. They spent the miles enjoying the countryside. Rose knew they were in a hurry, yet each mile brought them closer to ending this insightful trip together.

Back on the road, the day stretched out before her, Rose had time to think. Dinner with Mr. Geno had brought memories of her father forefront in her mind. She could remember all the good times. The times before talk of divorce. Her mind zoomed in to the chaos of the situation at home in Houston.

The family was derailing before her eyes. It was like railroad tracks splitting like a sort of switch yard gone haywire. As long as her two parents—like a train track with two runners—ran parallel connected by cross ties, that anchored them. It all running on into the future holding hands, then the family, like a train of many cars, followed faithfully into forever. The train was presently carried forward with a wild motion, but as one runner left the other, it was destined to crash into fragmented pieces. Inevitable.

Here before her, Anna, only 17, was ready to quit college and take care of her own future-Before it was too late. Who would follow? Rene now only 14, with bright intellectual promise and extremely talented as an artist. She was currently at the top of her class in a special art school. Definitely too young to take care of everyone. She was followed by Margaret, only 11 and after her Katerina who loved to dance, followed by Lily and her little brothers Rob and Tomas. All lived at home now. Smart, good-looking, talented, and bright. Most of them destined to be artists. All of them were full of potential. She anticipated bright futures.

Yes, Anna was right. If the two runners stayed true, the train that was her family would stay on track. But if her Dad and Mom remained split, she hated to imagine the outcome.

She knew no matter how much she wanted to help, she was merely a daughter, one of the children. She was not the parent. Rose by herself, or Muriel, or Anna, or Rene. No one could take the place of their father. He should be in his right place at the head of the table. He with stories told in his deep mellow baritone voice as he made them up; glancing at each of them as he lit his pipe, fragrant tobacco smoke billowing He was the rudder.

She had one faint slim wisp of an idea. Perhaps all they need do was tell him so. He was needed, loved, cared for, and above all-loved. Important to the stability of the family. All these daughters needed their father. As they all grew older and faced adulthood, they needed him even more.

As Anna and I are here together, perhaps we can visualize, imagine, speak our truth. The train can right itself, continue safely on the path to a wonderful unknown future.

The miracle was she could see the future and do what she could to set things right. But not alone. This was one thing she couldn't fix. Ultimately, she was a big sister, not a parent.

Anna and she danced and stretched by the side of the road. After a silent stretch, Anna spoke,

"Rose, can I ask you about something that had been bothering me for a while?"

"Shoot."

"We left Chicago when I was only three. I never got the story straight. Why did we move?"

"The mafia stole our house."

"Yes, I heard everyone say that. But how? Or Why? Don't you think that was the end of a lot of good things for our family?"

"I'm not sure. Why do you think that?"

"It's the way you and Muriel talk about everything. Like Deerfield, and the Chicago cousins, and even our grandmothers both still live there."

"Oh, yes. It was horrible. I lost my best friend. We left the piano. You can't carry everything in a U-Haul trailer when you leave in a hurry. The short story is that the banker, my dad's friend showed up accompanied by two hitman. They looked meaningfully at all four of us aged six and under. I think it scared our parents and they packed up and left everything.

"Dad wanted an extension on the loan, He had used the house as collateral. But it sucks. It really sucks. I grew up with that shorthand. 'The Mafia stole our house....' A statement I always gave as the reason we left Chicago. I had never really explored what that meant. The full ramifications for my Father and my parents."

"Well go on, we have nothing here but time."

Rose glanced at Anna's serious curious face. No time like the present. "Dad was an inventor as well as a photographer. He invented things to make the printing of photographs easier. He invented a machine to develop and print a role of photographs. He would laugh and say he put himself out of business, with that invention. As the process took over the mainstream photo industry, folks no longer needed to hire a photographer to print their photos and snapshots.

"He sold the invention to Kodak. He was paid for the invention. It was a lot of money to a 27-year-old with a family to support. But not the same as the kind of money you make when you patent an invention. He took the huge sum and bought his first home, it was almost half the price of the house. Then he started a new photography business in Deerfield. Our mom who had grown up in the slums of Chicago's south side was really happy they owned a home. My dad used the house as collateral when he got a loan for his new portrait photography business. His first business in Chicago was called Gabriel Studios. That is where I was born. My first memories were laying in a crib in the middle of a huge art studio.

"Once they bought the house, we were off to live in Deerfield, on the north side of Chicago just outside of Lake Forest and Bannockburn. Those are the happiest years of my childhood. Deerfield is my definition of happy; my best friend, Rita; the dead-end street lined with Linden trees; the horse pasture and barn at the end of the street. Even my trek across the field to Kindergarten. I met my best friend Jonathon there. A life of freedom. I walked all the way to town by myself when I was five. Happy parents, happy Christmases; Cousins; visits to family friends; and Sunday drives. When the Mafia called in the loan, before my Dad could extend it or renew it, the house was gone. Taken as collateral. Our parents lost everything. All of their savings were tied up in the home and business."

"I have since speculated about things. Like the fact that my maternal grandfather was supposedly a gangster. Was it more than just a bank loan? My uncle was in the penitentiary for dealing cocaine at the time. Were the underworld connections somehow rearing their ugly heads? Or was my Dad just to have horrible luck with business always and forever?

"As a kid you do not even know the right questions to ask. I just ended up leaving Chicago, my grandmother, cousins, neighbors, and we moved far away to the arm-pit of Houston, Texas. There we encountered strange small subdivisions of cheap housing surrounded by bayou's. I contracted a serious illness called *homesickness*. I was heart sick. I lay in bed every night. I couldn't sleep. How could our lives be destroyed so irrevocably?

"In my mind, that despair and bad luck, colored things ever after. Before Texas, and after Texas. I just longed to get back to Deerfield.

"Anyway, I am so proud of Dad, our father, for all he invented and continued to invent. He didn't quit or give up. He began a new business, Photo Murals. And also, Photo Design. He just never got the knack for making money at them. But not for lack of effort or inventiveness.

Our Mom just gets very upset at the hard work and time he invests in his business's yet always the lack of profits."

"I can understand now why I am so focused on making

money. Dad never focuses on money. He wants to do a good job. He wants perfection. No matter the hours he spends to solve the problem. Always searching. He is happiest that way."

"Happiness is important."

Finally, the last leg of the journey dragged on as they neared Paris.

It was almost midnight; Rose could see the Eiffel Tower all lit up in the distance as they approached Paris. The last ride landed them in the brilliant noise of the Eiffel Tower. Red and white taillights buzzed around the roundabout, at Place Trocadero as cars chased each other like a snake eating its tail. The Eiffel Tower glowed in the night sky. She could see straight down the alee to another monument, it too, aglow. Paris, the city of light. It was truly magnificent; powerful and mind spinning.

When their driver screeched to a stop, Anna thanked him quickly. Rose assured him they were fine. They jumped out, smooth as cats, as there was so much noise and traffic, and waved goodbye at the retreating vehicle. Rose grabbed Anna's hand, and they walked to a quieter side street to regroup.

"I don't want to disturb Edith and Jean at this hour," Anna said. Anna crossed her arms shivering.

Rose noticed her sister was thinner than ever. "Jean and Solange live near here. I recognize that street." Rose looked up and down the avenue, trying to get her bearings.

"Can't we ask someone?" Anna stated.

The two stood around a bit helpless. There were few someone's, and only random cars off the main roads. They headed east and walked a few blocks. They changed course and headed NW on another street. As they kept walking, and midnight was moving to morning, Rose quelled her anxiety for her sister's sake. It was her doing they had left the Riviera and now look.

Clearly, she had quickly become lost in the maze of Parisian neighborhoods. A tall man approached them out of the darkness. He walked quickly straight towards them. His blonde hair caught the light from a street lamp.

"Excuse est moi, mademoiselle, Quelle est le time?"

Anna turned on her heal. In a voice flat and cold, not at all like her normal self. She said, "I don't speak French."

"Neither do I, as it so happens, at least not all that well." The stranger spoke in a clear Midwestern accent, effectively shattering the somber mood that had settled on the forlorn travelers.

"You're American!" they both shouted in unison.

He bowed, "I am Ted. American as they come. I have been studying at the American Academy here. And who may I ask are you?"

"I'm Rose and," she looked up at her sister," this is my not so little sister, Anna."

"We're from Texas," Anna chimed in.

"What brings you —- what the hell are you girls doing wandering around Paris at Midnight? In this obscure neighborhood no less?"

AND SO IT WENT. THE THREE OF THEM BONDED THEN AND there. He took them to a late night café he frequented, as he knew the owner actually liked Americans. Ted was a perfect gentleman. He pulled out the little café chairs for each of them, settled their baggage behind the counter, and ordered café's all round. He placed his navy pea coat behind his chair, revealing clean khakis and a white button-down shirt. His straight blonde bangs made him look youthful and harmless. Suspecting the girls were hungry,

Ted ordered grilled cheese for everyone, and all became instant friends.

Rose wondered how old he was. "I'm a grad student," he explained, "with an exchange program here in Paris. This is my last night on the town, as it so happens. I love Paris at night." Soon he convinced them to join him in a last trip up the Eiffel tower.

Newly revived with coffee, relief, and the best grilled cheese anyone had ever tasted, both girls were energized and excited to attempt this trek.

"The lights of Paris at night. There is nothing like it."

"We've never done it. We had been staying with my aunt and uncle, and I am never allowed out after dark."

"It's settled then."

3 2
ANGELS

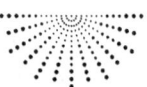

*R*ose hadn't realized how far they had walked since the car dropped them off. They really were in a tangle of old streets. Ted knew the way, so they trusted and followed. They turned left and right and right and left. All three busy chattering at the same time with the renewed energy of relief. They traipsed through the maze of skinny cobblestone streets, puddles glittering with light reflected from a street lamp.

The night went on, in a dream like way. They have no photos of Ted, as by then, they were exhausted, spent, and over it. Rose realized that the whole trip had been a sort of Act—a performance—almost a runway audition or a role. Now faced with a fellow American, the veil dropped, and they relaxed into being two kids, semi-runaways, eager to unwind and be themselves, once at the top.

What hit Rose first as she faced the city, was the wind. The night air was different up here. She braced herself, grabbing the cold steel rail as her eyes took in the scene. The city below was laid out like a map before her eyes.

The maze and tangle of medieval streets, cut through by long sharp diagonals that crisscrossed the city.

"I take it, you two aren't ready to impose on your family tonight," Ted said. "Come with me to the Student Housing. It's not far from where I met you two. I have plenty of room at my place."

Anna looked at Rose with a hopeful puppy dog look. Rose was still up for adventure. She squeezed Anna's hand and said, "I'd love to."

"It's been great to share my last night in Paris with you two."

Rose knew, by now, they would have followed him anywhere. Thus, Rose and Anna followed him. They crossed the Seine, strolled arm and arm through the Jardin de Trocadero. They followed Ted down Avenue Paul Doumer and he quickly darted back into the maze of side streets, that seemed so familiar to him. Finally reaching the large dark green painted wood doors, they followed him into the courtyard of the so-called student housing. Climbing two steep flights of stairs to his floor, they tiptoed through narrow corridors permeated with smells of lavender and musk. The high plaster walls curved into ornate ceilings. They passed rows and rows of closed mahogany doors.

He pointed to the black lacquered door at the end of the hall. "That is the ladies washroom, there are showers and everything. My room is this way." He opened the door to an elegant dorm type room, featuring a desk, a small sofa below a large steel window overlooking the courtyard. A sleeping alcove under an arch was tucked off to one side.

"Make yourself at home." He kicked off his Dockers. "I actually have a sleeping bag to offer you. I brought it for taking side trips on the weekends."

"And it's warm," Anna said, reaching out to touch the proffered flannel bedroll.

"Paris is not as hot as the south of France," Rose said. She noticed plenty of floor space and his blue down sleeping bag looked unused and cozy. "This looks perfect. You enjoyed being in Paris?"

"It was a lot more work than I expected. But yes. I loved writing and studying in the small café's, spending hours in the musty library, and taking walks in the Jardine des Tuileries, or walks along the Seine."

"I love the Seine, and so many parks. Lots of people kissing on the park benches." Rose blurted and turned red. What a thing to say to a stranger who offered them his room.

He smiled, "And lots of people watching along the Seine."

"With the artists on the banks. Yes, Paris is a wonderful City." Rose's face clouded, "I am sorry you are leaving just as we meet." Rose felt a pang at her sincere words.

Ted explained the drill. "You know, I have been thinking. You two want to be on your own in Paris. Anna is not so cool with the relatives. I have this place paid up until the end of the week. The room comes with these breakfast tokens. Which get you Café au lait, a baguette, and these little cow cheese things, triangles, wrapped in foil."

"I love those." Anna lit up. Rose could see she was about to drop.

"Are you sure? That would be great," Rose said. "It would give me a chance to show Anna, my Paris."

"Me too. And explore more," Anna said.

"So it's settled. I must leave early tomorrow morning. There are two keys, one for the courtyard and one for the room. No one will notice, this place is bustling during the day. Also, the staff is all students on separate shifts. It's different than a private hotel would be."

"What can we ever do to repay your kindness?" Rose asked.

Ted smiled, "I'm happy to help fellow Americans."

"I'm too tired to wash up tonight. I'm ready to tuck in. Hey, I thought your motto was to rely on the kindness of strangers?" Anna said.

"A Streetcar Named Desire," Ted said.

Rose thought he sounded wistful. "I wish we could have met earlier. I can barely speak French and you are the first American we've met the entire trip." Rose studied his all American healthy good looks, so different from Bernard and well, everyone.

Anna and Rose cuddled up in the one-man bag, into which they both fit somehow. Rose was filled with peace and gratitude. They had made it back to Paris, with plenty of time to spare. Listening to the night air, she was full of emotions she couldn't quite explain.

The last words spoken when all was silent, Anna said, "Ted? You are our Angel."

TRUE TO HIS WORD, THE NEXT MORNING, TED WAS READY. They must have woken up sometime near dawn as both girls were now on the single bed in the alcove. Rose had rolled up the sleeping bag and stuffed it into its sack. All books and papers, clothes and supplies, were gone now, tucked away. Ted hoisted his big backpack up on his shoulders.

Rose hugged her knees, "Thanks for everything Ted. Safe trip."

Anna was still asleep beside her. Early light was just peeking into the courtyard.

"Enjoy." He smiled in such a simple way, his white teeth glowing. An all American young man, Rose thought. Chivalry was not dead in Americans after all.

He shut the door behind him with a soft click. Lavender, and musk-like frankincense, swirled around her, as a puff of air left with him.

'*The poor will always be with you.*' Rose knew that quote from the bible. Were they the poor? Had they been the beggar's in strange countries as they went about their harmless adventure—-with lots of spirit, but little money?

'*The lilies of the field*'; '*The birds of the air.*' Blessings, blessings and abundance were being bestowed on each of these gentle, helpful, generous, people. People of the land; People of France. A catholic country made up of non-practicing Catholics. Ordinary people, that had shared their cars, bread, meals, houses conversations, dreams, and life stories with them, as they had traveled through the country like beggars. People are *Good*. Just like Karl Marx had said. But it must be freely given. What a disaster when generosity was forced.

Ted was somehow different. She knew he was their Angel.

Were all people somehow angels for each other? Angels for one another? Everyone had a soul. All the souls come from the same source. From the one True God. God *is* One. Everyone is connected. When we feel that connection we feel like we are in the presence of the Divine. Rose let Anna sleep in and went downstairs to find some breakfast.

PIANO MUSIC FILLED ROSE'S EARS AS SHE MOVED THROUGH the narrow corridor as if walking in a haze. Arpeggios trilled in a cascade of sound echoing from somewhere. What bright joy to wake up to on this new day. Morning thoughts, and now Music. Music fierce like tumbling waves. Where was the music coming from? Rose wondered as she stood in line with a scraggly group of people from everywhere, waiting for coffee and a baguette.

33
POEMS

ose carried the plastic tray with two café au lait, half of a crusty baguette, and a pat of butter, through the main hall and out to the garden. If Anna came down soon, she was prepared. Tucked beneath a tree she noticed a small wrought iron table. This was a perfect cozy spot. She sat down, taking in the morning, breathing the moist air. The garden was full of lush greenery. Small trees lined tall white walls that cloistered this haven from the city. The garden opened off a large room with a black and white tiled floor. There were huge arches over French doors that stood wide open to let the morning light and dove song in. From her spot at the table, Rose could just see someone at the shiny black grand piano. Trilling classical chords and arpeggios had followed her out here. She unwrapped the gold foil butter and watched a red cardinal hop in the branches as she ate her baguette. When Anna came down they would make a plan. In the meantime, a place to live together—on their own—was perfect.

Rose needed this alone time to catch up on her journaling. So much had happened that she was still spinning. Writing was her way to debrief and sort her thoughts. She idly sketched a few delicate ferns while she wondered how to frame her tumbled musings—and emotions. The garden had a few wrought iron benches scattered beneath a few of the larger chestnut trees. Brown fall leaves still piled up around the edges. The garden wasn't manicured at all, just a lush green abundance. She took in her surroundings as though she needed to remember this place always. She had some time yet, Anna needed her sleep. The crowds were inside in the dining room lined up at long white tables chattering away like birds on a wire. It's odd she was alone out here. She wasn't sure if she avoided people, or they her. She thought about her trip, pen poised above the paper. So much had happened. Where to start?

She had taken the train from Paris to Rome. On the train she'd spent hours watching life go by. Then she'd arrived in Rome. The day was indelibly carved in her.

ROME -
THE GIFT Of A STRANGER

330 beds in the castle lined the walls
In the huge room.
I, weary from travel,
Replaced by excitement
Of my first night in Italy.
Joined 200 back packers
With easy stories to share.
But no. Not for me
Not I. Not today.

My hostel card was not tucked in
The pouch with my funds and passport.
Gone.
Left perhaps in Norway
In my haste to move on.
Now, Rome was overwhelming.
Large and loud and crowded.
I had no place to stay.
Much to see, places to go
But no home base.

A red-haired stranger came to my aid.
He said he'd stick with me.
Escort me to find a place.
As the afternoon sun lowered
The sky glowed above red roofed villas,
A round fountain spewed water,
Glistened rainbow light
As it splashed, drenching bronze horses,
Their steely flanks bearing warriors.

I had a backup plan, a last resort.
To head to Vatican hill.
I could bunk with the Irish sisters
Who would take me in at their dorm like convent,
Once I arrived.
My new friend, stronger and wiser,
Than my 19 years said it wasn't far.
He would escort me through Rome
up to Vatican Hill.

I pictured a quaint small place.
With nuns in the cloisters

And Monks in their gardens all singing
A choreographed song.
Perhaps from the sound of music.
I strode with my friend.
Around each corner another magnificence.
The streets, maze-like in stone,
Spun me first to the Spanish steps,

I ran up and down,
feeling like La Dolce Vita.
Caught in the frenzied power
Of horses hooves, pounding water.
I did not bathe in the fountain.
Just beyond was the pantheon,
Statues by Michelangelo, Palaces by Bertolini,
Paintings by Leonardo,
Raphael Madonna's, hiding in a cathedral.

Somehow darkness seeped into the street,
We still roamed through the night.
Before us, the magnificent coliseum shone
Stone ruins of columns like gravestones,
Reminding us of all who had died.
The moon rose large and white,
Full as my heart at the sight.
The coliseum in moonlight
Spun webs around my legs.

I traipsed through massive stones
Architecture fallen over time.
White light on pale marble
Coaxed me through arched pathways and hidden
    corridors.
Mesmerized by time and distance,

My friend stuck through.
Until finally, up the winding path,
Thru the stone gates,
To the farthest section of the city on the hill,
The city within a city. Vatican Hill.
We spoke little,
I didn't know his name.
He let me take it all in with a grin.
Sister Mary Margaret unbolted
and greeted us at the door.
She welcomed me in, and turned away my friend.
No gentlemen allowed at a convent full of Nuns.
I was helpless.

I watched him walk away,
Into the night.
No hotels in sight.
I do not know his name.

WHILE STAYING IN THE CONVENT, ROSE HAD PLAYED THE piano daily. The sisters encouraged it. They rented some of the rooms to lay Catholics so Rose didn't feel too odd. They had set meal times three times a day. Back in her room after finishing a nice breakfast in the dining room after the early morning Mass. Rose decided this was the perfect opportunity to write a sort of Romance story—her first attempt at fiction.

Becoming a writer was her new goal. It was the perfect occupation for nomads. It soothed her gypsy soul to have a portable occupation. Architecture wasn't that. Real projects could take three long years. It was a stationary, sedentary sort of life. She would be obliged to settle some-where, eventually. In the meantime writing *if she could pull it off* was perfect.

Thus she began her first romance. Her characters were two gorgeous creatures—he dark and brooding, an architect with longish hair, and a sexy sullen female— facing each other. She had no clue what they would say or do. Her own pathetic lack of experience in the college romance department, had left her bereft of any vivid details or even dialogue. What do lovers say? She imagined they must make love all the time, night and morning. But she wasn't at all sure if that were true. Or what they would say, or even if lovers talked during it. She stopped took a breath and an hour later she still sat staring off into space, with pen poised above seven still blank pages. Rose realized she had nothing to write about.

However, she loved Rome as a city. She resolved to stick to art from that moment forward, deciding then and there to explore Rome. Her sketchbook became her constant companion. She marched off to the Medici chapel to sketch some well-muscled reclining nudes by Michelangelo.

As Rose sat in this beautiful Parisian garden, all of her earlier escapades came back to her. She considered her trip. All the new faces, and extraordinary time she'd had traveling with Anna. She was grateful she had sketches and watercolors and tons of photographs of their adventures. She thought of her time in Lourdes searching for a miracle. Bernadette's life had been one of affliction and suffering. All of which she'd offered up to Blessed Mary and the Sacred Heart. She remembered the story of Fatima, how Lucia had seen the sun spinning in the sky. And Blessed Mary prophesied the World wars. Virgin Mary proscribed what we all must do to end war—Pray the Rosary.

Rose wanted to follow God's calling in her life. Her greatest God given gift was art and architecture. One should develop ones gifts, it was a sacred pact, a way to honor God with your gifts. Architecture is a service profession. To create designs—schools, libraries, hospitals, airports—all for the public and helpful to society, is a service. In Rose's mind, bad building was a crime. Every footfall she placed in Europe instilled in her that all Europeans were committed to good, solid, or beautiful buildings. America hadn't got the memo before they started trashing the place with *Builder Specials*. Somehow they managed to destroy the precious landscape and pollute the resources at the same time. What a waste. Architecture was a sacred calling. She would fight hard for an education that would empower her to make a difference in the world.

Just that summer, standing in the embracing arms of Bertolini's piazza in front of St. Peter's Cathedral, she had seen the *Fuma Bianca* and John Paul II had become Pope. Saint Lucia of Fatima had foretold the attempted assassination on His life, in a message from Blessed Mary. Pope John Paul II had survived and become the *chosen one*. He was destined to make a difference as the leader of the Roman Catholic Church. The new Roman Empire.

ROSE KNEW AS SHE SAT THERE, THAT SHE MUST RETURN TO America. She must help her sister Anna find her way. And visit her mom and help out with the younger sisters when she could, between studies. Ah, here was Anna wandering in.

"I got some *café au lait* for you," Rose said as greeting.

"Good morning, what a beautiful garden."

"It is. Sit and relax. I'll check and see what other goodies I can dig up."

"Wait, this looks perfect." Anna tore a bit of the baguette off and began buttering it.

"Today we will have a day to explore Paris." Rose sipped her coffee. "I was thinking of the Louvre."

"Sounds musty," Anna wrinkled her nose. "I have heard a lot about the Avenue des Champs-Élysées."

"Champs-Élysées? There are tons of trendy shops there."

"Well I know you hate shopping," she teased. "What about the Musée de l'Orangerie."

"Well if you like impressionism better, we can go to the L'Orangerie."

Anna stirred her coffee and looked bored.

"Or we can take a day trip to Château de Versailles. The famous Palace of Luis the XIV and Marie Antoinette. It dates from 1682."

"Yes, I'd like to see that."

Rose looked thoughtful; "You know, Versailles inspired me when I was eleven. It was the first time Gramma Yvonne took me there. I was calculating how all of those rooms, with so many huge bedrooms, would make an excellent orphanage."

"Is it very grand?"

"It's absolutely amazing."

Each day, after breakfast and café au lait, Anna and Rose headed out and roamed the streets for another local adventure. At a nearby Chinese grocery, Anna bought rice along with two small blue and white bowls and spoons. The hostel let them cook their meal in the large commercial kitchen. During the afternoons between noon and 2:pm, the streets were quiet, and most shops closed for siesta. When one stall owner was lowering the awning, Anna noticed boxes of unsalable bruised peaches and pears tucked under the table. She managed to persuade the owner to give her the entire box of the bruised fruit for only a few francs. This was Anna's idea of a meal plan— rice, and enough fruit to get full. But it also kept them independent. Well fed and with a roof over their heads they were no longer at the mercy of strangers.

ROSE AND ANNA ENJOYED A KIND OF PARISIAN LIFESTYLE. Window-shopping was like eye candy. It didn't matter if one could actually buy all the clothes on display. Rose studied fashion with Anna by looking, much as she enjoyed art. She browsed through museums without buying anything. They had enough funds to stroll through the parks and enjoy a glass of wine in the Latin Quarter in the afternoons.

As they discussed the myriad of sites they could visit together, Rose recalled her favorite, Montmartre and Sacre Coeur. That was the best idea. The old streets of Paris, where the cobblestones told their own story. As an artist, she knew this could imbue Anna with another side of Parisian life.

It was afternoon as they ventured on the million worn steps that lead up to Sacra Coeur. The white Basilica's domes glowed against the deep blue of the sky. They strolled the alleys at the top, winding their way through narrow streets and worn wood buildings. Wood shutters creaked, the faded paint worn thin. A lone accordion player leaned against a wall near a gated park, the notes echoed in the evening air. A woman in a worn print dress stood in her balcony, smoking and watching the street as though waiting. A young man whizzed by on a bicycle, his groceries packed in his front basket. The stones glistened, shiny from oil slicks in the streetlights that had just turned on.

Rose nodded at the wood door to a bar. The neon light flashing pink. "Here is where they hung out. This is where they lived. On these streets. Some of the time. Can you feel it Anna?"

Anna smiled, "Yes, I think I can. Inspiration."

Rose nodded, "Yes. When we both are back, we can remember this place."

They stood together, holding hands, and gazed far off over the rooftops in the setting sun.

"Rose, we are so different. But I get it. I feel the vibe; history, not just that Brach and Picasso and Dali were here, it goes so much deeper and older. It's what brought them here in the first place."

"Mmm. And Toulouse le Trek, don't forget him." Rose said.

| 'Sacre Coeur'

Meanwhile, each morning in the quaint garden, Rose's pen found poems a daily ritual while she listened to the ecstatic efforts of the lone pianist. She knew the music was the classical repertoire. Bits of Chopin were interlaced with piles of arpeggios. It was as if their friend was composing on the fly, playing with an expressive exuberance. Rose didn't want to disturb his solitary efforts.

One minute she was in Rome. *Fuma Bianca*, what a blessing, to be present on the very day Pope John II was chosen at conclave. She'd taken a train with her Eurrail pass…

FUMA BIANCA

Traveling
in trains inspire me to stare
Out the window
As the train moves on.
I put my book down
Listening.
The rhythmic click upon the tracks
Are a metronome to memory.

Yet the landscapes out the window,
Of Italian trees and Tuscan hills,
Are so foreign to my normal
Site and sounds,
I now stare out at the past.
At the worlds of Michelangelo

And Saint Francis of Assisi.
I can see them just beyond
The red roofed stucco town.
Somewhere they are giving hope to the lost
healing the sick and clothes to the poor.
Or preparing an impasto
To adorn some forgotten Popes ceiling.

The Tuscan poplar trees, manicured cones
Like spires lining simple roads,
That lead to vineyards. And donkeys
Carry sticks, the old widow in black
Still uses
To light her fires in the night.

I find it strange.
That what you think about,
Like Michelangelo,
Seems still alive.
Ever present in your heart.
Like when I paint the figure
To paint and draw like him

Is what I strive for.
I wonder about his life;
His work; his pain.
The years upon his back with that ceiling
I never got to see. Because they
Were picking the Pope that day

Pope Saint John Paul II
In St. Peters square.
The oval to embrace the crowds.
'Fuma Bianca,' someone called,
'Fuma Bianca.'
The crowd went wild.

P A R I S AT L A S T

*O*ne morning, Rose was enjoying a second café au lait or was it the third? Anna had gone to get dressed in the room. Rose was *living one day at a time* and *being here now* and all the fruit they were dining on had made her feel a sweet contentment about life in general and these Parisian days in particular. She realized her story sounded a bit fictional. First, they were given rides all over France by kind men named Bernard until finally, they made it to Lourdes. Then Saint Bernadette herself had taken over and they had grown into new depth and under-standing. Then the angel Theodore had sponsored their last few days in Paris together. All in all it had been a wonderful adventure.

| 'Eiffel Tower,'

She had been to the American embassy and applied for the new emergency passport. She had also lost quite a few other things. Her big suitcase was at Aunt Edith's but to honor Anna's idea, they had agreed to lay low as if they were not back from their *supposed* train travels across the country.

She had not heard anything else about the gambler and the mystery surrounding Bernard and his dealings. All of that felt so far away now. What a sloppy traveler she was. As she had reminisced about her first trip to Italy and her shortened trip to Rome due to loosing her card, it dawned on her that perhaps it was careless to loose her hostel card, yet if she had it, she wouldn't have returned to Paris so quickly. Then she would not have found Anna.

It was their intuition that had connected them. It was their ability to read people that had saved them from bad guys but also made them feel safe around friends. In that sense she would remember Bernard fondly and not attach any dirty deeds to his character and tarnish her pretty memories. They were pretty thoughts. He lived in his jet set world of money and finance. Rose was too American for most Frenchmen it seemed, so her aspirations about being swept away by a handsome French suitor were dashed.

At any rate, come fall she would keep her date with Michelangelo's David. He was on a pedestal and she could admire him and sketch him to her hearts content. After Anna was safely on a plane back home, then she would see what came next. She was glad Anna would carry all the wonderful photographs and memories back home to her father's darkroom to be processed. It was her duty to return home too, but not yet. Just then Anna walked up looking lovely in the teal tank top and matching jacket Rose had designed and sewn for her.

Anna sauntered towards her in her model walk. She stopped and did a swivel turn. "I'm letting you borrow my clothes and we will go out on the town tonight. We are due another trip to the Eiffel tower."

Rose stopped her reverie and laughed. "I can't fit into your clothes."

"You can now. I have been a very good coach for you. You should see yourself!"

Rose laughed and shook her head. She'd been traveling and hiking and starving right along with Anna the whole time. It never dawned on her that she had lost a few pounds in the process. She got up and pulled up her loose jeans. "That sounds like fun. Do we have an escort?"

"Well, not exactly. But I have a plan. When we get to the top, we will find someone to take our picture. If we leave here by 5pm we will be on top at the golden hour." Anna pulled Rose up and marched her back up the stairs to their (Ted's) room. "Tomorrow we will go back to Edith and Jean's and they may even be happy to see us. But tonight it's just us. Girls rule!"

TWO YOUNG WOMEN IN COLORFUL SKIRTS AND JACKETS, ONE in Frye boots the other in sandals strolled through the high formal lobby, past the library full of books, and the black grand piano. The piano player stopped mid-stroke and looked up. For that split second between the chord and the trill, his hand poised above the keys, he glanced at Rose and her eyes sparkled as their eyes touched across the room. His hand came down on the e minor chord. Rose heard angels in the notes, the moment passed and the girls were gone into the twilight.

THE END

EPILOGUE

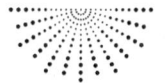

Rose in Florence

It was Late in September before Rose finally made the trip to Florence. She found a room in a dark Pensione. She had a quaint room tucked into the attic on the third floor. She was grateful for the cool room with white chenille bedspread on the dark antique double bed. She put her things quietly away in the drawers. Arranged her art supplies on the dresser. The day was dimming but a nice oblique light was slanting in from the one window. She sat at the vanity and faced the mirror, sketch book propped just so. She was here to learn from the masters.

Earlier in the afternoon she'd been to the Uffizi. She strolled past all of the artists under the arcade. Each was set up with easels and supplies for doing portraits. She quietly slipped behind the artists watching them work. One Renaissance styled man with a dark velvet coat and dark brown hair curling at his shoulders drew exactly like he could have been Raphael himself. She watched a long while, as his deft strokes in charcoal grew into an angelic face on the crème paper.

Now she chose a sepia charcoal pencil and posed her own face, half lit and slightly tilted before the antique mirror. She concentrated on both her strokes, the lighting, the mood and keeping her own face still. Yet her heart was hammering. She'd come to Italy to study art in her own way. Copying the masters techniques and images was valid. Yet under neath was the dim, slim hope that perhaps Bernard was out there too. Perhaps she could run into him as he strolled along the Arno. Or crossed the Ponto Vecchio. She caught the sparkle In her eye. The finishing touch on the portrait. Then in the distance, she heard the church bells chime into the white cloud sky. It was six o'clock. Not late at all. Perhaps time for an evening stroll. She could study the angles on the sculpture David that stood in the square. He stood proud and naked before all of Florence.

She hurried down the darkened stairs, hand sliding down the rubbed wood of the railing. The petite woman in black, head covered in black lace, emerged barely visible on the ground floor. "Arrivederci, senora."

Rose stepped out into the narrow street. As she approached the David she paused. People strolled swiftly in all directions, cars honked, pigeons flew. The grey streets reflected steely water from the days rain. The stone sculpture glowed with a blue light etching the features. David with his one arm raised to his shoulder, the other loose by his side. His stance tall and graceful. Her head cocked, her lips parted , her eyes wide—taking it all in.

And then a voice beside her. So close it was almost a whisper.

"At last, Rose."

She turned slowly, and there was Bernard. His face

broke into a grin. There he was, familiar, and friendly and not a stranger at all.

He took both her hands in his. "You look, you look... your face." He couldn't explain it. Instead he wrapped his arms around her. He held her hard.

Taken by surprise she let herself be held. Then finally wrapped her arms around him.

The End

Anna made her flight back to Houston
She became an interior designer after attending art school

AFTERWORD

As I write the last pages of this story, it brings to mind, yet again the lasting words of my great grandmother,

---

"you are only as young as your spine is supple."

I was told she had long black hair that never went grey. I always imagined her as some great gypsy fortuneteller. She fed people, she never saw a doctor, and she healed everything with home remedies. When it was her time to die, she called her loved ones to her bedside and said her goodbyes. Then she lay upon her bed and closed her eyes for the final time to sleep. She never awoke.

I often ponder the life of Amelia Lietze from Europe. She came from a world across the ocean, on a ship as a teen ready for adventure. What country? Why travel alone? A woman alone brings her daughter into the world, fatherless, although she is industrious and inventive. My grandmother Katherine gave birth to my mother Katherine, and she to us. All nine of us are here in America because one young 17 year old ventured alone on a ship to America in 1900. Yet, I too, now practice the Five Tibetan Rites. My spine is supple and my once silver hair is turning dark again.

Throughout my life, everything that came along – dance in the 70's, aerobics in the 80's, yoga in the 90's- anything that involved keeping the spine supple, I did it. If it swung, I tried it; Tango, Swing, Modern, Jazz,-not running which sounds like pounding your body—but twist- ing, shouting, Zumba, belly dancing—all the happy phys- ical expressions.

So when I received a letter from India, a letter in an ornate white envelope with many stamps, a letter that had traveled first to my parents, and then to me, at my various addresses, I saved it.

In it, the writer said that he had met my uncle—who keeps in shape as a mid-weight boxer and athlete—on his many travels. My uncle had spoken so well of me that this man determined to find me in America, and begged me to travel to India and join him on a particular quest. All that sounded quite impossible and unattainable at the time.

Only recently, upon rereading the letter, I observed the details. He had wanted me to discover the 5 Rites. So now in my garden, with all the time in the world to write, and think, and pray, in the monastery of my life as a married mother and grandmother—which means I am no longer traipsing the world in search of adventure—I am engaged in the 5 Tibetan Rites as a daily ritual. As it is passed on, with the wisdom of youth tempered by the experience of age, thus I pass it.

Michelle Moraczewski

NEW SCIENCE SALUTE

For further exploration:

Nikola Tesla
Born; July 10 1856, Smilan, Croatia Died:
*   January 7 1943, New York City, NY*
Nikola Tesla was a Serbian-American inventor,
*   electrical engineer, mechanical engineer, and*
*   futurist best known for his contributions to the*
*   design of the modern alternating current elec-*
*   tricity supply system. He had many inventions*
*   Including the AC motor, Tesla Turbine, and*
*   Carbon button lamp. In the 1800's, with his*
*   newly created Tesla coils, the inventor soon*
*   discovered that he could transmit and receive*
*   powerful radio signals when they were tuned to*
*   resonate at the same frequency.*

Noetic Sciences https://noetic.org
Institute of Noetic Sciences (IONS) is a research
*   center and direct-experience lab specializing in*

*the intersection of science and human
experience.*

*2022 Energy Science & Technology Conference:
Includes discussions of Nikola Tesla's thermody-
namic transformer, Advanced measurement
techniques for Tesla Coils, Also Tesla high
frequency illumination methods.*

*Edgar Cayce, Born: March 18, 1877, Kentucky,
Died: January 3, 1945, Virginia Beach,
Virginia
An American clairvoyant and medical intuitive.
More information about healing work in the
Association for Research and Enlightenment, in
Virginia Beach, Virginia. https://www.
edgarcayce.org/*

*Higher side chats
https://www.thehighersidechats.com/archives*

*Dr. Bruce Lipton
In 982 Dr. Bruce Lipton began examining the prin-
ciples of quantum Physics and how they might
be integrated into his understanding of the cell'
s information processing systems. His subse-
quent discoveries presaged the study of the
science of epigenetics.*

ACKNOWLEDGMENTS

I wish to acknowledge all the wonderful strangers who made this book possible, without whom there would be no story. Although this is a work of fiction, I spent time in the 70's hitch-hiking in Europe, America, and Mexico. I remember many faces but not names. I thank you all. The kindness and generosity of people remains with me to this day. Especially during these strange times when just a few years back we were taught to fear strangers; all wearing masks and staying 6 feet away. It's time to celebrate the goodness and humanity in our world. Our world is made up of people—human beings—holding, helping, feeding, and lifting one another up. We are not our government. We are all children of God, having a human experience. At this time, we are all in this together. In short, this story rests on the shoulders of so many. I also thank my large family and many friends who have encouraged my journey.

BOOKS BY M. MORACZEWSKI

Headwaters
   The Forgotten Tribe
   The Prophet's Lover
   A Creation Story
   Finding Wings, Poems
   Collections: Poems + Paintings

ABOUT THE AUTHOR

Michelle Moraczewski, author, architect, painter, planned to write just one novel, The Ranch Chronicles; a mystery-adventure set in the Texas hill country. Now she is going strong with her latest novella, Anna in Paris. She lives with her husband and a few horses, just an ordinary farm life in the extraordinary hills of Tennessee. Her lifestyle continually fuels her imagination.

Website: https://www.michellemoraczewski.com.
Website: fine art: www.mmoraczewski.com

THE PROPHET'S LOVER

Excerpt

Kahlil Gibran, poet, philosopher, and artist was born in Lebanon.Mary Elizabeth Haskell was born in North Carolina. Their meeting was profound. The story of their relationship is spiritual and passionate. Together their union birthed books that have impacted souls all over the globe. During his day he was beloved. August Rodin said he was the Blake of the Twentieth Century. Claude Bragdon wrote his power came from a great reservoir of spiritual life else it could not have been so universal and potent, but the majesty and beauty of the language with which he clothed it were all his own. Or was it?This is yet another tale of the great woman behind the man, the unsung hero, Mary Haskell.

CHAPTER ONE   1932

Mary's field of vision filled with the intense black charcoal that formed the eye in the saddest face she had ever seen; so much emotion in a single charcoal sketch—marks, careful and exact on thick rag paper. The face floated in the white background. The direct gaze of the portrait held her captive. Her eye filled with his eye. No, it was a sketch. Dark charcoal…

"I saw Jesus in my dream last night," his voice in her ear, intimate, probing. "The same warm face. The large dark eyes, burning peacefully. The dusty feet. The rustic, grey-brown garment. The long, curvy staff. And the same

old spirit, the spirit of one who does nothing but gaze quietly, sweetly at Life."

She could hear him as though it were only yesterday. Mary stood gazing, mesmerized at the eye, no, the soul of the man behind the portrait. Her eye was caught, her soul transfixed. All the memories came flooding back to her in a rush. She had been so smart back then. So poised, confident and sure of herself—back then. How long ago was that first show? How long had it been? As she stared, her mind flipped back in time to the first portrait. The first gallery show, was it 1907, or 1908? Back in 1907, she was in charge and in control of her destiny. She had been caught--transfixed that Sunday afternoon— by drawings in charcoal, ones much like these, every stroke seemed to vibrate. It had been more than 20 years ago she affirmed. She had been stunned at the charcoal portrait on view that afternoon. There were two drawings on the wall, she remembered. There were other paintings as well. It seemed like only a moment had passed since their first meeting…

BOSTON 1907

"Mary, Mary. Are you deaf?"

Gradually the words penetrated her consciousness. Mary felt the tug on her sleeve and turned to see her sister Louisa dressed to the nines. All Louisa's polish didn't improve her manners. She pulled Mary from her reverie back into the center of the room, where the gallery crowd grew steadily. Mary blinked and tried to focus on the sister that everyone called the pretty one, with her shiny blond hair, perfectly groomed. Taking her sister's cue, Mary resumed her role, which she knew only too well. As the headmistress of a school based on manners, it was her duty to make everyone feel welcome. Mary immediately greeted and

smiled at yet another face in the sea of Boston's faces—her
crowd.

Mary had accompanied her sister out this afternoon to a new
exhibit space in an old warehouse near the docks. It was all the
thing these days to appropriate unused warehouse space for
exhibits. The floor was concrete, and the ceiling had exposed
wood beams. The walls glowed white with fresh paint. The
paintings were rather traditional seascapes: oils of fishing boats,
water, and waves were prevalent, and some majestic landscapes
were quite agreeable. Yet, the moment they'd arrived, she'd been
immediately pulled, and had abandoned her sister, to study the
only two charcoal drawings. Mary marched right past the
seascapes and mountain views, mesmerized by the two drawings
on paper that hung together at the far end of the gallery.

www.ingramcontent.com/pod-product-compliance
Lightning Source LLC
Chambersburg PA
CBHW072209170626
46813CB00003B/859